·*·Girl·*·Writer·*·

Spies
and
Lies

·Girl··Writer·*·

Spies and Lies

Ros Asquith

PICCADILLY PRESS • LONDON

For Jessie, and for young writers everywhere

First published in Great Britain in 2008
by Piccadilly Press Ltd,
5 Castle Road, London NW1 8PR
www.piccadillypress.co.uk

Text copyright © Ros Asquith 2008

A catalogue record for this book is available
from the British Library

ISBN: 978 1 85340 954 7

1 3 5 7 9 10 8 6 4 2

Printed and bound in Great Britain by CPI Bookmarque, Croydon
Cover illustration by Bernice Lum
Cover design by Simon Davis

Set in 11.25 point Novarese Book and 10 point Comic Sans

Chapter One

Golden bikinis, gleaming metal stilettos, a turban glittering with precious gems. Drinks only champagne, eats raw egg. Paints her toy boys gold . . . Goldwobbler, Goldflinger, Goldfangle . . .

It was a week into the summer term and I was scribbling this inside my geography notebook under the beady eye of our batty new geoggers teacher, Ms Parker. I was thinking that, maybe, if I scribbled fast enough for smoke to start coming off the page, she would think I was a Keen Student pouring out my amazement at the Wonders of our Wonderful Planet. She's still amazed about all that stuff, which is really something when you consider she was probably born before the dinosaurs.

But all I really wanted to do was get back to my own proper writing, which was going to lift me out of dreary old Falmer North Comprehensive and on to breakfast TV. I was scrawling the character of the arch-villain of my fantastic new spy thriller, *The Girl with the Golden Pun*, starring Jane Bond, but the trouble was, it was the hottest first week of summer term in living memory and my biro was melting, and my green velvet dress – which shows that I am an original thinker and not a slave to fashion – felt like it was made of pulped porcupine stirred with glue.

'It's global warming!' bellowed Ms Parker, her gigantic round head nodding furiously like Noddy, so that her huge Planet Earth earrings bobbed up and down like the little bell on Noddy's cap.

Shame they're not bells, I thought. We could use the excuse to take a lunch break.

This always happened to me in school, especially when it was hot. I drifted into daydreams in which I was accepting the world prize for literature, maybe dressed in a green velvet trouser suit and red top hat. But I was brought back to reality with a jolt when Ms Parker heaved off her bizarre camouflage jacket (bit of a daft thing to be wearing that day) to reveal her emerald green T-shirt saying ECO-WARRIOR in enormous letters. Luckily, or maybe not, she is enormous enough to fill this T-shirt, which looked like the sail of a galleon in a high wind.

Before I knew it, my hand had shot up.

'Please, Miss, we're not allowed to wear slogans,' I said.

'*You* are not allowed to wear slogans,' she boomed, 'but as your teacher I have a vital educational message to put across. My slogan is not depicting violence, discrimination, profanity or vulgarity, but is a clarion call to save our beautiful planet. I see you've been taking copious notes, Cordelia.' (Help, she knows my name already. Maybe she's a good teacher after all . . .) 'Would you care to share them with us?'

'Oh, it's just, erm, scribble really,' I mumbled, feeling a red hot wave of embarrassment washing all the way from my toes to the short, scruffy, beige, mushroom-like mat that I call my hair. Ms Parker had put her quite considerable nose right into my book, like a bird digging for worms. Shame to have quite such a long beak with a name that makes it so easy to get called Nosy Parker, of course.

'Mmmm, *Goldflinger*, *Goldfumble*, *Goldwobbler*, what *can* this be?'

I thanked my lucky stars – and kind Ms Parker – for not reading out the bit about gold bikinis and toy boys, but of course I was awash in a sea of giggles from the whole class anyway.

'Please, Miss, it's word association,' whispered a little shy voice. It was Viola, come to my rescue as always. 'You see, Cordelia is a writer, and, like all writers, she uses word association to get her ideas going. Those words are obviously about the rich and greedy who are despoiling our beautiful planet,' said Viola in a rush. It was one of the longest speeches she had ever made.

'Yes, that's right,' I said, throwing Viola a look that I hoped clearly conveyed that she was my best friend in the universe and that I would walk on boiling poo for her sake.

Ms Parker smiled. With her strange combination of very round face and elongated Pinnochio hooter, she suddenly reminded me of the Big Friendly Giant.

'Well, I trust you'll put those skills to good use, Cordelia, because this term I am involving the whole of Year Seven in a fabulous global warming project. We are going to work on some displays for a very special parents' evening at which we will demonstrate how to save the planet! And we are going to do some real research for this. Proper grown-up fieldwork! Mr Frost has arranged to accompany us on a magnificent field trip at half-term!'

There were deafening groans at this. Mr Frost is head of PE, and he's obviously descended from the people who did the Spanish Inquisition. He makes people run round the field even when it's raining hard enough to wash you away. Jolene pointed this out to Ms Parker.

'Oooh, alas, that we might all drown in a spot of English rain!' she snapped. So she was just the usual type of sarky teacher after all.

'Will we go to the rainforest, Miss?' said Tobylerone.

He's named Toby, really, but he's tall and skinny with a triangular head so he's quite like the chocolate in some ways, except not very sweet.

'Or the North Pole? So we can measure glaciers melting?' asked Eric Cubicle, waving his ruler about excitedly. Eric gets excited about anything to do with measuring. There's a rumour he measured all the boys' willies in his primary school and put a list in size order on the loo door. This was apparently quickly removed, though whether by the boys at the bottom of the list or by teachers worried about Eric's future as a member of the community is hard to say. Anyway, Ms Parker said she wouldn't be taking the class to the North Pole unless we were all eccentric millionaires, but she wouldn't say anything else about the destination either.

'I'll tell you at the end of the lesson,' she said mysteriously. 'It's all about our carbon footprint.'

'Oooh, monsters,' said Eric gleefully.

'Yes, in a way.' And then Ms Parker told us all about how each of us has a carbon footprint, which means how often we use electricity or petrol or aeroplanes or fridges, and how each of us can do our bit to reduce it. We've all heard it about a million times before – but she still managed to make it sound interesting.

'I'd like you all to start keeping a diary about how much packaging you use,' she gushed, and then produced a whole bag of stuff that she said was an average person's packaging for a week. I was shocked. It contained burger cartons, pizza boxes, loads of plastic sandwich cartons and carrier bags and yogurt cartons and plastic bottles galore.

'We never use all that,' said snobby Sasha, whose mother doesn't let her eat takeaways.

'I'm glad to hear it, Sasha, but perhaps your house has different packaging: bags of salad, bottles of olive oil – who knows?'

Sasha looked thoughtful, but Ms Parker was drawing a huge picture of the world's carbon footprint on the whiteboard. Little Britain did not do too well on this map. It was embarrassing to think of how much stuff we've got and how little stuff other people have got.

Even the hoodies and banshees who smoke and cuss your mum were hooked by Ms Parker because she was so passionate, jumping around and flapping her arms like a flying Noddy. She was campaigning to get the whole school to recycle everything and said one of the best things we could do as individuals was to buy energy-saving lightbulbs straight away.

'My mum says they're well expensive,' Jolene said. Zandra agreed, as usual. Jolene went on. 'Easy for rich folk to make sacrifices, know what I'm sayin'? Anyway, global warming means we'll all be able to get a wicked tan just hanging out in the street, rather than stinking up the air with all them aeroplanes going to Benidorm an' that, so it's a good thing, innit?'

'Energy-saving bulbs last ten times longer than normal bulbs and are seventy-five per cent more efficient,' said Eric Cubicle, measuredly. He likes sticking to the point.

'Yes, Eric,' said Ms Parker gratefully. 'That's why they save money in the end, because they use less energy and last much longer than regular bulbs.'

She showed us pictures of the rainforests shrinking because they're being cut down and of glaciers melting and little wombat-like creatures that are becoming extinct and told us even tigers are at risk of dying out. Tigers! Oh no, we all thought, when we heard about the tigers – a world without tigers was not a world that we wanted. Even though we'd never actually seen them outside the zoo. But whether it was the tigers or the glaciers, I reckoned that by the end of the lesson the whole class felt really excited, so we didn't all rush out like a herd of galloping horses when the bell went. In fact, we all dawdled behind, except for Jolene and Zandra.

'So, are we going to Disneyland, Miss?' someone asked. 'Year Ten graphics went there to pretend to study design.'

'Did they, indeed? Certainly not. We're going to somewhere much more romantic and beautiful.'

'The Himalayas?'

'Italy?'

'Sorry to disappoint you all. It's Norfolk.'

Groan. Sigh. But a husky voice from the back of the class murmured, 'What's Norfolk?'

Everyone turned to look. It was the new boy, Vladimir Vyshinsky, already named Vlad the Lad, because he looks a lot more like Johnny Depp than most twelve-year-olds, but who so far had not said a word to anyone.

'He doesn't know where Norfolk is,' said snobby Sasha, at break.

'So? Where is it then?' said Jolene. 'And who cares? Anyway, he's not from round here is he? I reckon he's from Spain. Probably his dad's a bullfighter. Phwoooar. Talk about global warming . . .'

'Yeah. Think I'll do my project on him,' sniggered Zandra. 'Anyway, you're not catching me going to Norfolk. It'll be all mud and slime and we'll have to wear welly boots.'

'Eeeek, welly-boots,' shrieked Jolene.

'Haven't they got anything more interesting than boys to talk about? Anyone would think that's the only thing worth saving on the planet,' I said to Viola on the way home. 'I think this global warming project will be really fun. Nosy Parker's a lot better than our last geoggers teacher, who was all about colouring in maps.'

'Mmm,' said Viola, vaguely. She didn't seem to be listening. 'Look! There he is!'

'Who?'

Viola pulled me into the hedge.

'Vlad!' she whispered in awe, as if he was Jesus.

Sure enough, we'd just turned into my street and Vladimir Vyshinsky was going into the ancient crumbly block of flats just opposite my house.

'So that's where he lives,' said Viola, almost as though she had been thinking about nothing else all week. How boring.

'Ugh. I hate those flats,' I said. 'They're haunted. I've heard puddles of wee suddenly appear on the landings when there's no one there.' Viola looked horrified. 'Just joking. But there is a weird old woman with about five hundred cats on the ground floor. Callum and I used to think she was a witch.'

Viola ignored this.

'He's living right opposite your house!' she squeaked. 'And you never even noticed!' She looked at me in true amazement with her eyebrows all up high nestling under her fringe in an amazed way.

'What a pain, he'll probably want to walk to school with us,' I groaned.

'Do you really think so?' said Viola. 'I think he'll be too shy, like me.'

'Hope so,' I grumbled.

'Am I coming round to yours for tea?'

'No. Got work to do.' I really didn't want to listen to Viola going on about Vlad. And I stomped inside, thinking, is this it? Are my days of climbing trees and having fun well and truly numbered? Has it all got to be lip-gloss and girls' magazines about what shape you have to be, from now on? Has even Viola gone bonkers just because a boy looks about sixteen and has a husky voice?

No. That was just my imagination, surely . . .

And to prove it, Callum phoned the second I got in, demanding a meeting in the tree house.

'You're not going straight out again, are you?' wailed Candice. (That's my mum, by the way. I think I am the only person at Falmer North who calls their mum and dad Candice and Howard, but then I'm probably the only person to have parents called Candice and Howard. All right, I know I'm lucky to have two whole parents at all, who actually live together, even if they have got silly names.)

'What about your homework? Have you fed Xerxes and Blue? And what about your writing? You'll never get your book finished if you go out playing all the time.'

This is typical of Candice – she always thinks three reasons are better than one to stop me having any fun. I threw some food into Blue's fish tank, feeling guilty as usual because he looks so lonely swimming around on his own. It's a point of principle with Candice that I feed him, even though it takes half a second to do. And Xerxes too, who is too fat and lazy to forage in the wild and murder little mice and birds like sensible cats. I think he needs an exercise programme actually. Maybe I could do a pet exercise DVD to fund my career as a novelist.

Candice likes the idea of me being a writer but says I'll never make any money from it. I point out to her that I actually have an aunt who makes loads of money – Laura Hunt, who's a famous writer of books for young people, although she doesn't write about exciting things like I do, about romance and adventure and spies and stuff.

I love Aunt Laura and I'm always looking up her writer's tips for inspiration, but, if I'm honest, I get a bit bored by all the 'issues' she writes about and I'm not that sure how good she is really. Maybe it's Candice's snobbery affecting me. Candice wants me to write Great Literature. I don't think she'd be crazy about Jane Bond. All I've told her so far is that it's an action-packed contemporary drama, which seemed to satisfy her.

I spent so long trying to find a bowl for Xerxes, rummaging around the barmy collection of Candice's homemade pottery that accumulates in our kitchen, that Callum rang a second time to ask where I was.

'Bowls,' I said to him, still rummaging with one hand. He knew what I meant.

Finally I found a shallow thing that looked like a small canoe with horns on it. Everywhere you look there are daft unusable coffee pots shaped like the Empire State Building and jugs made like pianos and you can never find anything useful for your Weetabix. Anyway, I emptied two tins of Chat Supreme into this thing.

'You know this stuff costs two pounds ninety-five

pence a tin!' I squealed at Candice. She's always moaning about money and how Howard never gets a decent pay rise for his lectures and teaching and stuff and how nobody appreciates art and literature any more, but she has absolutely no idea how to shop. Anyway, I rinsed out the Chat Supreme tins and put them in the recycling box, feeling a smug glow.

'Maybe we should let Xerxes forage for his own food, like cats since the Dawn of Time,' I pondered out loud.

'He'd starve,' said Howard, who'd just come into the room, looking even more like an absent-minded teddy bear than usual. 'He can barely stand, let alone hunt. Mice would play practical jokes on him.'

'You should hear what Xerxes says about you,' I told him. 'Anyway, I'm off to meet Callum. I won't be long.'

'Don't go near the playground,' shouted Candice as I left. 'They've cordoned it off – something nasty in the paddling pool. Chemicals, I think.'

I wasn't really paying attention to that then. But I would soon.

Callum shouted down something extremely grumpy from the tree house as I clambered up through the leaves. Cheek, since it's usually him who's always late.

But as I yanked myself through the narrow entrance, the leaves making me scratch myself all over like they always do, I was shocked.

'What have you done?!'

The whole tree house had changed. Callum's dad built it for him out of an old garden shed when he was six – so it's got windows (broken) and a roof (leaky) – and it's been like a second home to me ever since. We've had midnight feasts and all sorts of games and plots and adventures up there. He had somehow heaved a battered old sofa into it, hung a curtain and even rigged up some electricity in there so he was sitting playing Nerdzapper Seven on a laptop when I arrived. (It's a game where you have to spot the geek in a crowd of millions and 'take them out' before they infect the rest of the population with brainy ideas. Don't know why Callum likes it; he is that geek.)

'Callum, you can't play computer games in here, it's sacrilege,' I said. It was as though another layer of innocence had been stripped away.

I sat down with a big flump on the broken sofa. 'Ouch!' I yelped.

'Sorry about that spring,' Callum said. 'I found the sofa on a skip. But I thought you'd like it if I improved things a bit.' He was looking hurt now. 'You said we were too old for tree houses.'

'I didn't. Did I?'

'You did!'

'Yes, but that was when we were starting secondary school and trying to be all grown up. That lasted just one term. Then we came back here, remember? And realised we still needed it.'

'Well, we do. But now it can be a study, or . . . or . . . a studio. You know, for you to write your books and me to paint. It'll be like old times . . . but different.'

I was touched now. I could see Callum had kept some of the old stuff: the shelf with a toy horse of mine on it, and some ancient model cars. And the aged treasure chest we lugged up here when we were nine, crammed with emergency rations in case we ever needed to run away. I realised that Callum wanted to go on having it all just as much as I did, but he'd transformed it so that now he could say to his folks, or his new friends at his posh school, that he was going to his studio. Maybe that's what grown-ups are doing really, when they go into their sheds. It's as if everyone needs a tree house in some way . . .

'It's good,' I finally admitted. 'I will be able to write up here. It's . . . inspiring.'

Callum relaxed.

'How's the new book going? What's it about?'

'Ah. Glad you asked,' I said, whipping out the first chapter. Callum is still my greatest fan. 'This one will be truly excellent for you to illustrate, because it's all boys' stuff, although of course with a woman hero.'

'You're so sexist. Anyway you mean heroine.'

'Sexist yourself. Heroine sounds like a drug. Why not hero? Women are called actors these days, and poets.

You wouldn't say poetess, would you? This hero's a secret agent, 0007, Jane Bond.'

'Hmm, I see many possibilities,' said Callum, twirling an invisible moustache like a pantomime villain.

'She's James Bond's younger sister, twice as daring as her famous brother, but modest – so though she's saved the planet from destruction countless times, nobody has known about her until now.'

'Cool! So I can draw her car: the full mistress-spy works: jet-propelled Aston Martin complete with retracting chariot-style scimitar wheels, ejector seats for unwanted passengers, a bootful of starving piranhas, a homing device . . .'

'No, Callum! This is my story. I want to tie it in with my geography project; we're doing a really important thing on global warming. So I think Jane Bond should drive a pink Smart car, to minimise her carbon footprint.'

I hoped to impress Callum with the carbon footprint thingy, but he knew about it already.

'Don't be ridiculous! Spy stories have got to be power-ful, thrilling and packed with gadgets. You'll be having her on a stupid push bike next.'

'What do you mean, stupid? Bikes are good! Cheap, quiet, don't mess with the ozone layer . . .'

'Yeah, but if you drone on about the environment and health and safety, your readers'll just throw the book away and put on a James Bond DVD. What are you going to do, have her telling M she'll have to go by rowing-boat to the rendezvous in the Bahamas because planes are bad for the atmosphere? Refuse to chase the evil mastermind if it involves going faster than twenty miles per hour in a built-up area? Remind a hitman to be careful not to run with his knife facing upwards? It's all ridiculous. You can't have a book like this without explosions and poisoned umbrellas and car chases and underwater nuclear devices and —'

'Oh, it's hopeless talking to you about it. You can't know what it is to be a writer.'

Callum's ears wiggled madly, like they always do when he's angry or upset, or even thinking very hard.

'Sorry, I didn't mean that, exactly . . .' I started.

'Oh, you didn't mean my dyslexia? Well, at least I can draw,' he said sulkily.

'Sorry, Cal. I can see you've got a point about it being exciting . . .'

'Yeah. A mountain bike with wings and flame throwers and —'

I whacked Callum with my folder, full of my fantastic hand-written story (I'm using a fountain pen and purple ink just now as it feels more creative than the computer).

'Hey, slow down, only joking. Obviously the environment is the big thing in schools because I'm doing it too. My art teacher says I've got to enter the "Young Artists Save the Planet" competition. He says I'll win.'

'Of course you will; you're a genius.'

Callum opened his jacket to reveal a T-shirt, which said, I *have nothing to declare except my jeanious.*

'It's a quote from Oscar Wilde, you know, that bloke who wrote *The Happy Prince.* He did lots of great adult stories too, like . . . er . . .'

'I know,' I said. 'He wrote *The Picture of Dorian Gray* and *The Ballad of Reading Gaol.* He was put in prison for being gay.'

Callum's ears went ballistic.

'Prison? Just for being gay? When?'

'About a hundred years ago, but it still happens in some countries.'

'No! Does it? Will people think I'm gay if I wear this?'

'Honestly, Callum. Who cares if you're gay? But there is one thing about the T-shirt . . .'

'I know it's the wrong spelling. It's the dyslexics' version.'

'Should I make Jane Bond dyslexic? Brave as a lion and crafty as a fox but can't read maps, and takes wrong turnings in the final few gripping pages where she's hunting the nuclear bomb that's going to blow up the world?'

'Too many messages. But you do need nuclear bombs. And poisons. And weird deadly things. Like in the playground.'

'What?' I asked, forgetting Candice's warning.

'You know, they've cordoned it off.'

'The one in my road?'

'Yeah, haven't you noticed? It's got some sort of weird deadly thing in the paddling pool. How come you didn't see it?'

'Too busy watching Vlad.'

'Eh?'

So I told him about boring old Vlad and how he lives in my street and how I don't want to have to walk into school with him, because the banshees would never leave me alone. And how everyone fancies him, even Viola.

'Even Viola?' said Callum, his face falling. 'What's Vlad short for?'

'Vladimir.'

'That's a Russian name,' Callum said. 'His dad's probably a spy. Or maybe he's a spy himself.'

'Russians don't spy any more. They're all into hair products and wide-screen TVs now, like everybody else. But maybe that's just a blind . . . Vlad *is* very interested in chemistry. Hang on a minute . . . '

'What?'

'You know the weird deadly thing in the paddling pool?'

'Probably a shark,' Callum suggested.

'No,' I replied, remembering what Candice had said. 'It's something chemical. Toxic chemicals, geddit? That playground is right next to Vlad's flat.'

Callum looked at me and I looked at Callum.

I'll leave you for a moment at this dramatic point of

realisation that we had a spy in our midst, and share the first chapter of my amazing Jane Bond book. If only I could decide on Goldflinger/Goldbungler/Goldwobbler's name.

Laura Hunt's Top Tips for Budding Writers:
At the beginning and end of each chapter try to have a little drama so the readers can't wait to find out what happens next.

Hmmm. How about, Jane Bond hung by her teeth over a vat of boiling piranhas, or In ten seconds the world would explode . . . but those ten seconds were ticking away.

The Girl with the Golden Pun

'A medium sweet martini, with a slice of lime. Stirred, but not shaken.'

Secret Agent 0007 Jane Bond's husky yet musical voice echoed in the cavernous cocktail bar of Miami's richly carpeted, heavily chandeliered premier casino. Bond swept back her long, silky, golden tresses, which were shiny enough to rival the dripping gems that encrusted the hordes of rich old women who surrounded her, and adjusted her prominent cleavage, casting a languid, thickly-lashed eye over the barman. Cute, she thought, as she took in his svelte form in its nicely fitting, tight little barman's jacket and even tighter barman's trousers. But a man should be a mirage – something you can flick on and off, like a light switch.

The smell of smoke and sweat in a casino is repulsive at two in the morning, and Bond knocked back a few martinis to steady her nerves, for she had been waiting at the bar since midnight to catch a glimpse of the notorious Aurelia Goldflinger, whose devious gold smuggling had reputedly made her the richest (and most vilest) woman in the world. Not content with that, Goldfumbler was now threatening to destroy the whole human race.

Bond sipped her fourth martini, her eyes combing the roulette tables.

She cast her mind back to her last meeting with her spymaster, the brilliant and masterful head of operations known only as Z, whom she had seen in London just two days before.

'The Secret Service holds much secret information that is kept secret even from the most senior officers in the organisation,' Z had said, secretively. 'Only my chief of staff and I know absolutely all the secrets there are to know. He is responsible for keeping the top-most secretive-secret record of all, so that, in the event of the death of both of us, the whole story would be available to our successors. All you need to know for now, Bond, is that Aurelia Goldflinger is currently not only the richest but also the most dangerous woman on the planet. She has informed us that unless we hand over the entire gold reserves of the British banking system, the Chinese government and Fort Knox itself, she will unleash a nuclear device that will shatter the whole Earth! We believe that you, Bond, are the best qualified to track her down before she destroys us all . . . You will recognise her instantly, for she wears only a gold bikini.'

'I like an enemy in a bikini. No concealed weapons,' Bond had remarked, her triple agent's brain alerted to the prospect of a new challenging challenge, although her usually cool exterior was belied by a droplet of sweat forming on her elegantly-shaped right eyebrow and threatening to trickle down her high sculpted cheekbone on to her full mouth, coated in just a hint of Caprice lip-gloss 'for women on the move'. She had seen much action in the past ten years, but, at just thirty-two years of age and looking, as all men said, much younger, the glamorous agent was wondering whether she'd had a touch too much danger and might just pack it in and get an allotment. She betrayed none of this to Z, however, who now appeared to be entrusting her with the future of the entire human race in its entirety.

'Am I to do it alone? How?' Bond had enquired, her full pouting lips set in a grim line.

Z looked frostily across at her. 'Matter of fact, 0007, I had the Treasury on to me only this morning. Their liaison chap thinks that the Triple-O section is out of date. Here's our chance to prove them wrong. Goldbangle is going public with her threat in six days' time, or is it seven?' Z cast around his desk for an old calendar.

'Every calendar's days are numbered,' Bond had quipped, wondering whether, at ninety-eight years old, Z was still the man for the job.

'Ah, here it is. Yes. Six days. If Goldbungler's threat is made public, then there will be worldwide panic. We'll either have to give in to her demands or she will blow us all to smithereens. Naturally, we cannot take that risk.'

'But if she blows up the Earth, what's in it for her?' Bond had asked. 'Surely she too will die.'

'This is what's in it for her,' muttered Z, pointing to his laptop. 'She has built herself a planet, orbiting our moon.'

'A planet?' expostulated Bond in amazement. It was like something out of those far-fetched books about her brother, James. Could it possibly be true? Jane Bond craned forward to gaze at the tiny golden orb circling the moon.

'She has been planning this for the last decade.' Z grimaced, scorn dripping from his every word. 'She has used her immense wealth to buy the services of the world's top astrophysicists and rocket scientists to create this new world for herself. She has gathered supplies for a thousand years and a hand-picked army of extraordinarily handsome young men to cater to her every whim, and she has, in her underground cave, two thousand slaves who will run the planet for her. She has been kidnapping them from Romania, Ghana and Uzbekistan . . . One of your tasks will be to free these unfortunates, who are chained in darkness awaiting their fate.'

'The very handsome young men?' Bond whistled through her straight white teeth, her tongue flicking fitfully over her full, sensual lips.

'And the slaves,' said Z, sternly.

As Z gazed at Bond, the grim expression on his rugged, weather-beaten face folded in on itself like a wedding cake left in the rain. He had seen too much horror and had sent too many agents to certain death over fifty years. Bond was a young woman, she had her life before her; maybe she would want a family one day. 'Of course, Bond, if you feel unable to take this task on . . . If you'd rather live long and quietly rather than live fast and die young . . .'

'They say you only live twice. Once when you are born and once when you look danger full in the face. Why squander my days in trying to prolong them?' Bond responded.

Z smiled. 'I knew you'd do it. You'll need this.'

Z handed 0007 a briefcase full of essential spy

gadgets and a file. 'Your contact in Miami is Hunky Misterson. Good luck, Bond.'

When she'd left secret service headquarters, Bond felt hot and cold all at once. She knew she had no choice but to find this monster and stop her at all costs. The allotment could wait!

Laura Hunt's Top Tips for Budding Writers:
Every writer is different, but I find I'm never happy until I've got a splendid title!!

Have so far tried Licensed to Drill (*in which Jane Bond disguises herself as a dentist to infiltrate Goldflinger's lair*), For Your Pies Only (*in which Bond pursues a cannibal baker who puts his victims in pies*) *and* Doctor Maybe *where the villain can't make up his mind how to kill Bond. But I think* The Girl with the Golden Pun *says it all.*

Chapter Two

In the couple of days after Viola and I had spotted Vlad's flat, I got phone calls from Jolene, Zandra, snobby Sasha and five girls I'd never even heard of, all wanting to come round to mine or pick me up so we could walk to school together. News travels fast and they all wanted to spy on Vlad. Even Little Lucy, who lisps and is small enough to hang-glide on a Pringle. Viola was round at my house every night. She said she was really into this global warming project and wanted to do a big book with me.

'Would you have time to do the drawings for us, Callum?' she asked, while we were all sitting in my room drinking hot chocolate from china boots.

Callum sighed. He'd do anything for Viola, but he was obsessed with his own young artists' project and his mum was forcing him to go to a million dyslexia tutors so he could keep up with the work at his posh school. He explained he only got a place there on some sort of arty award for drawing, and schools like that don't go a bundle on dyslexia.

Viola wasn't listening anyway. She kept finding excuses to wander over to my window and stare out at Vlad's block of flats. The weird thing was, we'd never seen him in the street since that first day. Maybe he'd got an underground tunnel into his flat that led to the school – and perhaps to the poisoned paddling pool. And who knows where else?

'Isn't it lovely you've made so many new friends?' said Candice brightly the next morning, as yet another unknown girl rang up asking herself round. 'That Sasha sounds like a lovely girl.'

When Candice says someone sounds nice, she means they don't sound as if they come from a council estate. She was against my being friends with Viola because she lives on the Duchess Estate. Local do-gooders are always campaigning to demolish the Duchess and even I don't really like going there; it's all rubbish-infested dark alleys full of muggers and wee. I realise I'm a bit of a snob myself, but I couldn't help saying, 'Sasha is the most dreadful snob, actually. She won't talk to Viola because she lives on the Duchess.'

Candice blushed. 'Oh, I expect that now Viola's father

is . . . free, they'll move out. Just as soon as he's back on his feet.'

I drowned my Weetabix in milk, sulkily. I didn't like to tell her that Viola's dad still hasn't got a job. It seems like you get punished twice for going to prison – once when you're in there, and all over again when you come out and nobody trusts you with a job – even if you were innocent like Viola's dad.

'Look, I know you'd prefer me not to go round with all the hoodies and banshees. I know you wish I was at the posh single sex school, meeting nice girls whose parents do "interesting things". But you don't earn enough money for that, do you? So here I am and you'd better get used to it.'

'All I said was that I was glad you'd made some nice friends,' Candice replied sadly.

I felt mean, so I changed the subject by telling her off for buying bottles of mineral water.

'Don't you realise it costs zillions of quid to fly that stuff round the world? And packaging it is rubbish for the environment? And it's not even any better for you to drink?'

'Oooh. Sorreee,' she said, biting back. 'Your bedroom's a bit of an ecological disaster come to that. Have you heard of a wastepaper bin?'

'A recycling bin, you mean. And we haven't even got any of those energy-saving lightbulbs. It's pathetic,' I said. I could hear what a prat I was being, but I couldn't stop myself somehow. I get so fed up with Candice always wanting me to do better.

'Howard doesn't mind about who I hang out with or what I do, like you do. He just lets me be myself.'

'Oh well,' sighed Candice, looking tragic. 'Maybe it's because I'm a mother. Fathers don't seem to worry like mothers do.'

'Look, if anyone calls, just say I've had to leave early,' I shouted, panicking at the thought of banshees pounding up the path. I shot out of the door, guilty about Candice's disappointed face and feeling doubly guilty about lonely Blue, flapping his lonesome fins at me from his shelf in the hall.

I went the long way round to school. The thought of having to walk in with all the banshees linking arms with me and pretending to be my best friend just so they might get the chance to drool over Vlad gave me butterflies. On the way I kept noticing chewing gum on the pavement, old burger cartons, chip wrappers blowing about, horrible fumes from lorries . . . I was so busy tutting to myself at the state of the planet I didn't notice I was crossing the High Road until someone grabbed me and pushed me violently into a bush.

'What are you doing?' I squawked, as my school bag went flying, scattering its contents all over the road, including my precious Jane Bond story.

I nearly plunged into the path of a lorry trying to rescue it.

I looked up to see who'd pushed me over. It was Vlad.

He watched for a minute as I scrabbled around retrieving my precious pages. He took a step towards me but I threw him such a filthy look that he stopped dead and didn't say a word. When I looked up again, he'd vanished.

I saw him scurrying ahead as I turned the next corner. Why'd he pushed me over? What if I'd fallen under a lorry instead of a bush? I could've been killed! I tried to remember what had happened. Had he pulled me, or pushed me? I shivered. I had a strong author's instinct about Vlad. My Aunt Laura, the fabulously successful author of *The Terrible Twins* series, as well as even more books than Jacqueline Wilson, is always going on about the 'authors' instinct'. She says authors have a special way of seeing the world. But she also says my imagination tends to run away with me sometimes like, erm, a runaway lorry . . .

Well, my author's instinct about Vlad was that he is an Evil Force.

Viola ignored me all morning and didn't even sit in her usual place in the front next to me in English, where we are 'Parsing's Pets' because the brilliant English teacher, Ms Parsing, believes we are going to be Great Writers one day.

'What's up with you?' I asked, finally cornering Viola in the loos.

'Nothing.'

'You've been avoiding me all day. Do I smell?'

'No.'

'No really, come on Vi, spill the beans . . .'

'Don't call me Vi, Cordelia Lucinda Arbuthnott. How many other moronic names have you got?'

So that is how our conversation went on – a series of pathetic insults. Why is it that when someone is cross with you they can't just come out and say why, but prefer to sulk instead?

I decided to concentrate on higher things and went to the library to read about global warming.

But the dreaded Vlad was in there taking up a whole table with scrawls of chemical formulae and there were loads more on the computer that he was glued to. He saw me, pretended he hadn't, and turned the computer monitor off so I couldn't see what he was doing. Hah! Probably looking up more chemicals to poison kiddies' paddling pools.

Everywhere I went I ran into him. It was weird. And he was always by himself. Why didn't he act normal and make some friends?

This thought made me realise I'd been at Falmer North nearly a year and my only friend was Viola and she'd gone off me. I had a peculiar sensation that I was going to cry. Vlad turned round to see if I was still there, and his face looked like a storm-cloud when he saw I was.

I fled to the loos. Maybe I should just live in the loos, like that moany ghosty girl in Harry Potter.

The day went downhill after that. Nosy Parker made us split up into groups of three to do our projects and put me and Viola with Vlad!

'I think your gentleness and serious approach, Viola, and your imagination, Cordelia, will help him flourish. His English isn't very good and he needs support.'

'Oh no,' said Viola, which cheered me up for a millisecond until I realised it was me she didn't want to be with. Nosy Parker looked distressed.

'Please don't tell me I was wrong about your gentle nature, Viola. That's not a very charitable response.'

'Oh, I wasn't saying no about V . . . V . . . Vlad . . .' Viola stuttered.

'What then?' Nosy Parker demanded.

'I . . . er . . . just remembered I hadn't fed my goldfish this morning,' Viola said. Nosy Parker looked relieved. Zandra and Jolene, who were so interested in this conversation they were practically sitting on Vlad's lap, burst into action. By chattering at a million words a second, that is – their mouths are the only action-muscles they ever use.

'Miss, Miss, they might die, Miss, and it'll be all your fault! We'll be in the group while Vi goes home!'

'Don't be ridiculous, she can't go home,' snapped

Nosy Parker. 'What do you think this is, a holiday camp?'

'Don't call me Vi,' muttered Viola.

Vlad looked bored.

'We've got work to do,' he said.

'That's the attitude,' said Nosy Parker brightly. 'On you all go then.'

Nosy Parker finally hustled Zandra and Jolene off to the other side of the classroom (from where they kept casting the kind of hot looks at Vlad that were probably worsening global warming by the minute) so the three of us were alone.

The rest of the lesson was well embarrassing. Viola kept simpering and showing him all the stuff we'd been working on together and asking his advice. She kept flicking her hair at him and fluttering her lashes. My toes curled into my sandals. He didn't seem impressed, which was something. But he wouldn't look at me, which was something else. In fact, without looking either of us in the eye, he just kept on talking in this strange, growly, monotonous voice. It was like having the radio on.

'Water,' muttered Vlad, clenching his fist and staring at it. 'That is everything. You are water, I am water. The world is water.'

I tried to catch Viola's eye, but she wouldn't take it – or the other eye, for that matter – off mad Vlad.

'We cannot live without it. But we cannot live with it. If we do not stop destroying the planet, it will rise up and drown us. And we will deserve it,' Vlad went on. I was getting tingles in my spine. Viola was probably getting the same, but for different reasons.

I realised the class had gone quiet. Tobylerone, at the next desk, winked at Vlad and raised a bottle of mineral water to his mouth.

'Cheers,' he said.

I didn't see him move, but Vlad's hand whacked the bottle out of Tobylerone's grasp so it flew across the classroom and hit Eric Cubicle in the ear. 'Ow!' Eric said patiently, and started scribbling in his notebook, probably working out the bottle's acceleration.

'Cool it, man,' Tobylerone said.

'You're right!' shouted Vlad, triumphantly. 'We all have to cool it! That is our mission as citizens! You drink mineral water? You crazy! Water is everywhere, and you heat the planet up by pouring it through factories, and sticking it in plastic bottles! My father says sometimes he thinks the human race doesn't deserve to survive! I agree!'

Vlad fell silent, scowling to himself. Viola and I moved our chairs back a bit.

Eventually Nosy Parker broke the ice. (This is not a reference to global warming and the North Pole, but a famous writing term; as you can see I'm always keeping in practice.)

'Vladimir, you should be a little gentler on the human

race. But your passion for this subject does you credit. You're a person after my own heart.'

She came over to us, globe-earrings bobbing, nose slicing through the air like a ship, terrifying smile on her face which was meant to be really friendly.

'I expect great things from you three,' she said. 'Viola's common sense is earth, Cordelia's imagination the wind . . . and Vladimir's conviction is . . . the fire . . .'

She drifted off, still smiling madly. Vlad fell silent after that, and scribbled formulae to himself. Viola and I stared at our notes, pretending to read. I couldn't wait for the lesson to end.

After school the banshees descended.

'Isn't it enough for you being Parsing's pet? Trying to be Nosy Parker's too?'

'Vlad don't like you anyway, said yer were so ugly yer'd make blind kids cry.'

'And so dumb the only way yer can make up yer mind is putting lipstick on yer forehead.'

In my room. Miserable. Told Candice I wanted to go to another school.

'The banshees are horrible. Vlad's nuts. Nosy Parker's nuts. Viola hates me.'

'Oh, poor darling, are those rude girls bullying you?' she said, her face all agonised as though I'd told her I'd got a week to live. I immediately regretted it.

'Only joking,' I said quickly, with my best fake sickly grin. 'I love Falmer North.'

Just then the doorbell went. 'Say I'm out,' I shouted after Candice.

'But it's Viola,' she called back.

'Tell her I don't want to see her. Say I've gone to . . . Russia.'

'Don't be silly, darling, Viola says she's come to say sorry. Have you two had a row?'

So Viola came in all meek and sweet with a box of violet chocs – my favourite. She said she understood how I was feeling because all the banshees had been having a go at her about Vlad.

'But you've been horrible to me, too,' I wailed.

'No, you've been horrible to me. You haven't walked to school with me all week.'

'That's because I've been trying to avoid them,' I said. 'And him.'

'Oh. Well you don't have to worry about that. He doesn't want to do the project with us anyway. I heard him ask Ms Parker if he could work alone. He got all agitated about it and she said yes.' Viola looked miserable, but I cheered up.

'Oh goody. He's a pain.'

'Why don't you like him?'

'He's so weird. He's in a world of his own, and he doesn't want anyone else in it. And there is something creepy about him. Maybe he's a psychopath. Honestly Viola, I think he tried to push me under a lorry.'

'*What*?'

'Well, I don't know if he meant to . . . exactly. But he nearly did.'

Viola went very quiet.

'You shouldn't say something like that unless you know it's true,' she said. 'Why would he do that? I don't think you believe it yourself, do you?'

'I don't know,' I said. And I didn't.

'Anyway,' she said. 'We're too young to let a boy come between us, aren't we?'

'Let's hope we never get that old.' I gave her a hug.

Viola's eyes drifted to my window again though, searching for a sign of Vlad. It seemed she just couldn't help herself.

'Ohhh, that's weird,' she murmured.

I joined her at the window. A huge tanker had arrived outside Vlad's flat. Square men in fluorescent jackets were dragging big pipes towards the house.

'It's got one of those toxic chemicals signs on it,' Viola said in awe.

'That proves it, then, doesn't it?' I said.

'Proves what?' asked Viola, but she was hardly listening.

'Oh, nothing,' I said, put off by her tone of voice. I realised that to tell her I thought Vlad was a poisoner was a step too far.

She lost interest in the action outside.

'I don't mind you not liking him, you know,' she said to me. 'But it's not his fault all those stupid girls chase him. And he's brilliant about all that environmental stuff. He really cares about it.'

'Hmm.' I had to give him that.

'But really, Cord,' continued Viola, 'you shouldn't go around accusing Vlad of things you might be wrong about, just because he annoys you. He could get into real trouble. Look what happened to Dad.'

'Well, that was terrible,' I said. 'It's horrible to waste away in prison for something you didn't do . . .'

'He didn't waste away,' protested Viola. 'He kept himself very fit.'

'You know what I mean. But this is different. Vlad is really weird to me. I don't want to be near him, and if that hurts you, I'm sorry.'

Viola looked as if she was going to cry. I put a hand out to her.

'Look, let's not fall out over this. Walk to school with me. I'm going to go in late to avoid Vlad. You could keep me company.'

'No I can't,' Viola said. 'The school's getting stricter every week. If you're late they send your DNA to MI6 or something. My mum doesn't want two people in the family with criminal records.'

So Viola went home looking sad, and for the whole

next week I trailed in late to stay out of Vlad's way in the mornings.

Candice nagged me and my excuses became more and more feeble, from finding it hard to wake up ('Oh you poor dear, it's probably a growth spurt'), to losing my watch in a bizarre gardening accident ('I'll get you a new one on Saturday, that My Little Pony watch was a bit babyish, wasn't it?'), or claiming Xerxes had eaten my homework and I was trying to coax it out of him with a mouse on a string. She saw through this last one and I was relieved. The guilt about her being so nice about my lies was beginning to get to me.

Sure enough, on Wednesday I got a late detention and on Friday there was a sarky letter from the head of Year Seven.

'It's because I can't take my usual short-cut past the paddling pool,' I moaned, 'because someone's poisoned it.'

'Nobody's poisoned it,' said Candice, her kindness stretched to snapping point. 'It's some chemical imbalance. But I've just had a thingy through the door telling us all to use bottled water for a few days to be on the safe side in case it's affecting our drinking water.'

'Really? They've poisoned the drinking water too?'

'Nobody's poisoned anything. You're also changing the subject. I don't want you to be late for school once more this term, do you hear?'

'Right. I'll have to leave an hour early then.'

'Are you trying to avoid someone?' said Candice, kindly. But it was that sort of kindness that comes with such a truckload of worry that I just couldn't confide in her. I've got to prove to myself that I can handle this.

I didn't know who to ask for help except dear old Aunt Laura, world famous author of *The Terrible Twins*.

```
Dear Aunt Laura,
There's a bad boy, Vladimir, in our
school who all the girls fancy. Even my
best friend, Viola. He lives over the
road and everyone wants to walk to
school with me just to catch a glimpse
of him. But I need time alone to think
my thoughts. I am fed up of being
teased about him. Also, I think he's a
criminal. What should I do?
xxC
PS Love to the Three Bees and Joan and
Joan.
```

The Three Bees are Auntie Laura's manic grandchildren who seem to spend half their lives in hospital for drinking bleach and the rest being babysat by Aunt Laura so she only has time to write one book a week instead of two. Her cats, unimaginatively for a writer, are both called Joan.

Still, even if she can't find decent names for her cats, I've got to hand it to her – she e-mailed me straight back.

Darling Cordy,
Of course you need time with your thoughts. All writers do.

The fuss about this boy will die down soon. It always does. Then things will return to normal.

I wouldn't think he's a criminal just because everyone likes him!!!! What is your evidence?

Why not talk to Callum about it?

Let me know how you get on.

Big hugs to Xerxes from Joan and Joan.

Aunty Lolly xxxxx

I was round at Callum's straight after school on Friday and poured it all out.

'I wouldn't mind having some of what Vladimir's got,' said Callum. 'What makes him such a babe magnet?'

'He's tall for his age, his voice has broken – no offence – and he looks . . . sort of dark and interesting, I suppose. Some people say he's like Johnny Depp. Shows how blind some people are.'

'Hmm,' said Callum, waggling his ears, which made

him look about eight. Callum has not had his growth spurt and, for the first time since I can remember, I am taller than him.

'Still,' he said, 'even though Vladsky's boringly tall and hunky, I don't really see quite what you've got against him.'

'Well, first, there's the pond being poisoned. That happened just by his block of flats.'

'Sorry to interrupt, 0007,' said Callum in his best Spy Master growl (although unlike Vlad, he still speaks with a squeak). 'But we've no evidence yet that the paddling pool has, strictly speaking, been poisoned . . .'

'Well, someone's obviously tampered with it or they wouldn't have cordoned it off,' I said. 'He's always snooping about in the library looking up chemical stuff, and he went bananas the other day and started going on about how the human race doesn't deserve to live.'

'Why?' asked Callum, looking interested.

'Because . . . because we're destroying the planet with all our waste and junk, and . . . and . . . drinking bottled water instead of turning on the tap, and . . .'

'Aha!' shouted Callum. 'Proves you're wrong! If he was poisoning the water supply, what would it make us all do?'

'I don't know,' I said. 'Die, I suppose.'

'Drink bottled water, you noodle,' Callum said. 'The very opposite effect to the one you're saying he wants.

It don't amount to a hill of beans, 0007. Though of course . . .' he leaned over now, looking as if he was about to reveal a big secret, 'his family could be importing mineral water from mysterious Russian hot springs. He'll be opening a revolutionary new night club and spa soon, complete with fiery cossack dancers.'

Callum was obviously unconvinced Vladimir was a Sinister Presence in our midst. So I played my ace. I told him Vlad had tried to push me under a lorry.

Callum whistled.

'That's bad. You should tell a teacher. Or a hitman.'

'Yes, but I can't prove that's what he did.' I heard Viola's voice in my head, telling me off. 'It all happened so quickly . . . But why push me? Does he know I'm suspicious of him?'

'Hmmm, it does sound awesomely suspicious, I suppose, when you put it all together like that. Maybe he's really sixteen and has been planted in Year Seven by an international ring of saboteurs and he's planning to poison us all and take over the world . . .'

But Callum was interrupted by the loudest noise I've ever heard.

BARROOOOOM!

A tremendous explosion rocked the tree house, shattering the remaining window. We flung ourselves to the floor, quaking.

Seconds later, before we'd had time to speak or think,

there was another almighty bang and a dazzling flash of light. Then a loud, loud silence. You couldn't even hear a bird, or a rustling leaf.

Time stopped.

I thought, We are the only people left in the world.

Seconds, or maybe hours, later, everything seemed to happen really fast: there were shouts, the wailing of sirens and images flashing across my mind at triple speed like an old silent black and white movie. Candice . . . Howard . . . Viola.

I jumped up.

Callum was already on his feet. We stared at each other in shock.

Callum sprang to the shattered window as if he'd been electrocuted.

'Mum! Dad!' he shouted.

'Callum! Thank God! Is Cordelia with you?'

I stuck my head through the jagged tree house window. Callum's mum, Andrea, was tearing down the garden towards us, clutching her mobile.

'Yes, she's here, she's fine.' She was gabbling into the phone. 'Yes, come and get her.'

Shakily we climbed down the ladder and fell into Andrea's arms.

Apart from a long funnel of smoke at the corner of the street next to the playground, the world was normal. Andrea made us hot chocolate and, for once, Candice's look of anguish when she arrived a couple of minutes later was something I felt grateful for.

'Was it a bomb?' I asked as soon as my teeth stopped chattering. And, believe it or not, a part of me was thinking this will be good for my writing – I've understood at first hand that your teeth can chatter from shock and fear, not just from cold.

'Nobody knows, but they've gone on full terrorist alert. There are armed police all down the street. A couple of kids were hurt but nothing serious. Thank goodness the playground was cordoned off.'

'Why?'

'Seems the explosion came from that block of flats next door. Blew out a room on the top floor. No one in it luckily, but it all came down right on the swings and roundabouts. Just imagine if that had been full of kids . . .'

We all shivered. Vlad's block of flats.

I looked at Callum.

He looked back.

Suddenly this was serious.

That night I looked out of the window and saw, outside the cordon the police had put round the building, a hooded figure lurking. I could swear it was gazing up at Vlad's flat . . .

The Girl with the Golden Pun (ctd)

'You can go a long way in Miami with a few grunts. "Hi!",
"Uh-huh", together with "Sure thing", "Guess so", "OK,
boss" and "Ooh, you're too wealthy for me, but I'll go out
with you just this once!" will do for everything.'

Hunky Masterson was telling Bond all she needed to
know about acting the dumb blonde. He had met her off
the plane and was driving her to her hotel. Bond found
her eyes drawn relentlessly, as if on strings, to his
blond hair, chiselled chin and long legs encased in
Armani 747 jeans (stonewashed). All Z's men wore suits
and ties, so Hunky was a nice surprise. Bond liked her
men a particular way. Golden hair. Dark honey eyes. A
sinful mouth. Perfect figure. And of course they had to
be confident and witty and know how to dress and play
chess. Naturally they also had to know how to make a
perfect omelette. By the looks of Hunky, he seemed to
be just her type.

'First, the gadgets,' said Hunky as he swerved
smoothly into the palatial car park of the Miami Ritz. 'I
know that's what you triple-0 agents like best. Walk this
way.'

'I'll try,' said Bond, smiling to herself as she strode
after Hunky's wiggling hips and into a lift that seemed to
descend into the very bowels of the Earth.

'What do you think?' asked Hunky, with a wink.

'That'll do nicely,' riposted Bond, running her long, firm manicured hand silkily down the wing of the immaculate battleship grey Aston Martin Vanquish DB Mark III that Hunky had provided for her and wishing, as she did so, that she was running her hand down his long firm thigh.

'This Vanquish is customised to become invisible if you need it,' said Hunky, flicking his tousled blond mane. 'It's all done with mirrors.'

'So it's an Aston Martin Vanish then,' joked Bond, arching an elegant eyebrow. 'What else does she have?'

'Oh, the usual – retracting chariot-style scimitar wheels, ejector seats for unwanted passengers, a bootful of starving piranhas, a homing device . . .' said Hunky, running his eyes shyly over Bond's cleavage. 'And of course you'll need this. It's the same model as Goldfangler uses.' Hunky handed Bond a gold plated Smith & Wesson 45.

'It can, of course, be disassembled into a pen, a torch, a Swiss Army knife, a thing for getting boy scouts out of sticky situations and a cigarette case. And, naturally, as well as firing gold plated bullets, it doubles as a standard issue dart gun using both cyanide and explosive tipped darts.'

'Only four people I know of use such a gun. I believe I've killed three of them,' Bond replied, raising a seductive eyebrow.

Hunky gulped. He longed to run his muscly hand down

Bond's slinky tresses. But that would have to wait.

'I'm afraid there's no time to lose. Aurelia Goldfumble is due at the casino at midnight. You must watch her every move – we have traced her operations to a warehouse in Geneva where the white-gold armour of her Rolls-Royce Golden Ghost is regularly being melted into aircraft chair-frames, to be smuggled into Burma. It is there, we are certain, that she has an underground cavern . . .'

'Filled with slaves and a device capable of blowing up the world?'

'I see that Z has told you much. But has he told you about the mechanism to defuse the bomb? The mechanism is . . . Oh Jane, Jane . . . You are even more beautiful than I thought you would be. Will you kiss me passionately when this mission is over?'

'Yes, yes, twenty-four hours a day. Now, go on about the mechanism.'

Bond gazed quizzically at Hunky, admiring once again his finely chiselled jaw and shiny biceps as he described in minute detail how to defuse Aurelia Goldshoulder's bomb.

'It is worse than you think. Goldshoulder has already set the timer. It is to explode in three days, thirty-six minutes and . . .' Hunky glanced at his rolled gold rolliflex watch, a thin bead of sweat running down his well flexed muscular forearm, '. . . and forty-eight seconds.'

'Never mind the seconds,' said Bond, snapping into action. Both Hunky and the allotment would have to wait. 'Where can I find her?'

'She and Dr Midas, are always at the casino from midnight till four a.m.'

'Dr Midas?'

'Midas is Aurelia Goldbangle's one-legged, steel-toothed, metal-rimmed bowler-hatted, bayonet-booted, ruthless sidekick and hired assassin. His cruelty knows no bounds.'

'I trust he is broadening his talents by studying chemistry at night-school?' queried Bond, her lip curling in scorn, for she had defeated many more scary-sounding opponents.

'Domestic science.' Hunky smiled. 'He's a part-time chef. Recently he had an argument with Goldwarbler and in retaliation he cooked her beloved cat in a pie. He said the cat was nosy and had it coming.'

'Curiosity killed the cat,' remarked Bond.

'Goldflinger killed fifty of her slaves in a rage, when she found that Zanzibar was missing. But she never knew he had been cooked in a pie and that she herself had eaten him. Nor that Midas was the culprit. However, I intervened, with a Trojan Cat . . .'

'A Trojan Cat?'

'Yes, you know, like the Trojan Horse. Z sent me a perfect replica of Zanzibar, a sophisticated robot cat wired up so that we now know every move that Goldwarbler makes.'

Bond gazed at Hunky with even more admiration than before, turning this information over in her capacious spy's brain.

'There is no time to lose,' she yelled. 'But first I must change.'

Hours later, she reappeared, encased in a gold leather trouser suit, her slinky tresses flowing free.

'She'll like me in this,' she said, sliding into the Aston Martin.

'Wait!' shouted Hunky. 'There's something else I must tell you!'

But Bond had put her foot down and powered away into the heart of Miami, leaving Hunky gazing helplessly after her, his heart fluttering like a trapped bird against his manly chest.

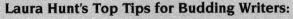

Laura Hunt's Top Tips for Budding Writers:
Try to get to know your characters well before you start. Jot down things about them. Then you will find that they have adventures with very little help from you, almost as if they are writing the story themselves!

This does not work. It's obvious who Jane Bond is. She's just like her brother James. But so far I've been sitting here for two hours and she hasn't written a single word for me.

Chapter Three

Laura Hunt's Top Tips for Budding Writers:
Use vivid language if you can. No clichés!
Your writing should be bright as a button.

Or sharp as a pin? I rest my case.

'They're saying the explosion was a gas leak but obviously it was Vladimir. He must have been making a bomb and something went wrong.'

'Well, if he was, he was doing it at the top of the building because his flat and the ones beneath are fine. Dad says they built houses better in those days, no one's even been moved out.'

'Well, that just goes to show how clever he is . . .'

Callum and I were spying on Vlad's block a couple of days later. The police cordons and anti-terrorist squad had vanished and instead a group of guys from the gas company were standing around scratching themselves and clutching mugs of tea.

'What are they all doing?' said Callum, yawning. We'd

been spying for two hours and he was bored.

'Waiting for a drill.'

'Why does it take six of them to wait for a drill?'

'Howard says two are waiting for the drill, one is telling them to wait for the drill and the other three are replacements in case the first three get sick. He says they can charge more for six.'

'Hmm. Wish I could hire six guys to do all my work, and six clones of me to go to all these boring tutorials . . .' said Callum lazily. 'And you could hire six writers while you just lounge around eating cherries.'

'Hah! I've got an idea!'

'Yeah?'

'Remember that bit I'm writing in Jane Bond about the Trojan Cat?' Callum looked blank. I've stopped expecting him to be quite as enthralled by my stories as I am, so I went on regardless. 'You know that weird old woman living in the ground floor of Vlad's block? The one we used to think was a wicked witch?'

Callum nodded absent-mindedly. He seemed to be straining to see something.

'Well, I think the old witch is Russian too! She's got a funny accent and her name's Ludmilla something. They could be connected.'

'Yeah. So? How does that help? Where's the Trojan Cat come in?'

'She's got zillions of cats, hasn't she? They drape

themselves all over her like a fur coat. We could, um, borrow one – pretend it got stuck in the tree house . . .'

'What, and stick a tape recorder in it?' asked Callum, suddenly remembering my magnificent plot device.

'No. That would be cruel. I mean we could pretend to rescue it and then call round. We could get into the block of flats that way!'

'Yeah. Good idea. But take a look at that.'

I followed Callum's gaze and saw, for the first time, in the window of one of the flats opposite, Vlad himself.

He was holding a long cord in his left hand and was weaving about in a weird way – bending and straightening – as though he was tucking it under something.

'It's just like that Hitchcock film *Rear Window*. When the photographer sees a murderer through the window . . .' said Callum, his eyes alight for the first time all day.

'Dunno what you're talking about,' I said.

'He's tying up a body! Obviously!' said Callum, his ears flapping like windmills.

'Lordy, do you think so?' I pressed my face to the window.

Vladimir was ducking and weaving with the cord. His other hand seemed to be pulling and pushing. Callum was right. I was sure of it.

'We must phone the police,' I hissed.

'We need a better view,' Callum hissed back. We both felt that Vlad could hear us. We charged up to Howard's study in the attic. I'm not supposed to go in there without knocking but we hurtled in anyway and Howard woke with a start, scattering papers everywhere and muttering that he was trying to finish an important article and what did we think we were doing?

'Sorry, Sir,' said Callum absent-mindedly, in his best posh public school voice, which made Howard even more bemused.

'Sorry, Howard. Got to look out of your window,' I said.

'Not more explosions, I hope,' muttered Howard, fumbling for his glasses as we crouched by the window to get a better view of the murderous Vlad.

I'm glad we did take a second look before dialling 999, because Vlad was not tying up a body. He was doing the hoovering.

'Sorry, false alarm,' I said to my bewildered dad and we half ran, half fell down the stairs, guffawing.

'Oh, he's obviously not a terrorist,' I gasped, as Callum and I flung ourselves on my bed and the giggle fit subsided. 'Who ever heard of a terrorist doing the hoovering?'

'I'm surprised you, a writer, can say a thing like that. Of course terrorists do hoovering, and shopping and all sorts of other everyday things. They even go to jobs and smile at people. You don't think they just live in a box labelled *Terrorists: assorted* and pop out like jack-in-the-boxes when it's time to blow something up?' said Callum. His pride was wounded because he'd made the stupid hoovering mistake, but it wasn't that stupid really. Try it yourself – if you can't see the hoover it does look very like someone tying up a big bundle . . .

But what he said got to me all the same. I suppose I don't like to think of terrorists doing ordinary-people-type things. I imagined a terrorist smiling at me. It was weird to think that someone could seem quite ordinary and be doing terrible things. I had an image of Hitler eating a jam sandwich. I felt tired and sick.

'Never mind,' said Callum, sounding genuinely disappointed that Vladimir had not committed a murder this time. 'We can still prove to Viola that Vladimir Depp is not all he seems . . .'

I tossed and turned that night, thinking of Hitler as a baby, eating a boiled egg and maybe looking cute. Maybe I'd been wrong about Vlad. Maybe Callum only wanted to trap him because of Viola. Maybe I was just jealous because Viola likes Vlad and Callum likes Viola.

At two a.m. I was wide awake. I padded over to open my window and gasped. There was a figure lurking by the paddling pool. Someone had climbed over the cordon and was kneeling down, staring into its depths (not that it's very deep, of course). The figure took something from its pocket – a bottle or a flask perhaps! And sure enough, dipped it into the water. I strained to see more clearly through the gloom but I couldn't make out the figure's face, since, thanks to global warming, our council has streetlights of about ten watts. I'd just decided to slip outside and creep closer when the moon, a full one, sailed out from behind a cloud and illuminated the figure of – Vlad! His face was pale, his eyes glinting caverns beneath menacing bushy brows, his mouth contorted in a vile grimace of triumph! He looked exactly like a vampire. Vlad the Impaler!

Next day, I knew I had to tell Viola. She'd been taking Nosy Parker's advice seriously and offering to help Vlad with his English every spare minute, although so far he'd always refused. I had to let her know that she might be assisting him in evil deeds. I texted Callum for advice on the way to school, but as usual I forgot his posh private school starts ten minutes earlier than ours, so his mobile was off. I decided to take matters in my own hands but, just my luck, Viola and I were split into different groups for maths and science. Falmer North has taken to putting kids in different sets so that the top ones soar away into Oxford or somewhere and the rest are left to fester, just another step on the road to turning us all into robots. Because Falmer North is a 'failing school' the head has been trying to 'turn it around' and weed out disorder. Naturally, Vlad and Viola are both in the top group for maths and science whereas I can barely tell the difference between a number and a symbol. Alas! What hope for me, sitting with all the hoodies and banshees slamming desks and being written off as thickos.

To my increasing alarm, I couldn't find Viola at break. We always go into the quiet corner of the playground at breaktime so we can have a good moan together. But where was she today, just when I really needed to warn her about Vlad? Come to think of it, where was Vlad?

I'd got so wound up by lunchtime that I'd begun to think he'd abducted her, so I was relieved to find them both in the library, but angry to see them sat next to each other with Viola giggling and even grisly Vlad grimacing in what looked very nearly like a smile. Even Hitler patted babies on the head, I told myself as I marched up to them and demanded to know where Viola had been at break.

'Out!' hissed the librarian, pointing me furiously to the door. It was the long skinny librarian with metal teeth. Not my lucky day, as the usual librarian is quite cuddly and likes to show you her hamsters, which she keeps under her desk. Even the library is turning into a police state.

'But she was giggling!' I said outraged.

Viola looked betrayed, but it did me no good anyway, as she was allowed to stay and I had to leave. Supposing I had needed to look up some vital facts, or even just read a book? You never seem to see anyone doing that any more except in wonderful Miss Parsing's lessons.

Other teachers just make you read little chunks of books and compare them to other 'texts'. If it wasn't for Miss Parsing – and Nosy Parker – I would leave school. I stood at the door gesturing wildly at Viola but she didn't look up once.

'What were you doing with Vladimir in the library?' I bristled on the way home.

'I was helping him with some weird chemistry. I didn't understand a word of the chemistry but he needed help with some of the English. Anyway, what's up with you? You're like a bear with a sore head. You're not starting your periods are you?' she added excitely.

'No, I am not. You're just like Candice. She always thinks if I'm in a perfectly reasonable bad temper that it's because I'm tired or hungry. Soon it will be periods, too. I hope I never have them!'

'Sorreee,' said Viola, who started her periods at primary school and occasionally likes to pull rank about it. 'But be careful what you wish for.'

'I suppose you mean I may never have babies. Well, I don't want babies. I won't have time to be a Real Writer if I have babies. Anyway all that stuff in the library was just because I really needed to talk to you.'

Viola stopped. 'I need to talk to you too,' she said, linking arms, 'but you go first.'

'Let's leave it till we get back to mine,' I said, glancing

round. Sure enough, the usual gang of banshees was a few paces behind. Jolene caught my eye and did a little cossack dance with her arms crossed and her legs shooting out at right angles. Quite impressive for someone whose idea of exercise is opening and shutting her mouth. They all fell about.

'It's driving me bonkers,' I whispered as we turned into my street, 'I've got to talk to you about, about . . .'

'Is it Vlad?' asked Viola.

'Yes!'

'Me too. I've been desperate to tell you . . .'

We sneaked upstairs avoiding Candice's stream of questions. 'Did you have a nice day? How was geography? Did those awful banshees bother you? Did you remember to hand in your chemistry?' and on, and on . . . I wish Candice would spend more time at her gallery instead of hanging round worrying about me. She used to be so busy when I was younger but now that I'm nearly a teenager she seems to think I need a parent who's always at home checking up on me.

Viola waded through my room absentmindedly matching socks and folding things as she went.

'You're very tidy, for a dreamy person,' I told her.

'I have to be. You can't swing a mouse by its tail in my place.'

Viola has a sofa bed in the living room of their tiny

council flat. She has no space she can really call her own, which is probably why she loves our big chaotic arty house so much. My own room's quite small, but, even though it's bigger than Viola's front room, you couldn't see a single centimetre of floor.

'I'm having a big tidy up at the weekend.'

'No! I love your room! Don't change a thing! It's so . . . free,' and, without knowing she did so, Viola drifted towards the window and gazed in the direction of Vlad's flats.

'About Vlad . . .' I started.

'Oh, yes, I've been longing and longing to talk you,' said Viola.

'Me too. I just didn't know how to start. I've been so worried . . .'

'Oh, you shouldn't worry, really. I suppose I knew you had your suspicions . . .'

'I've been suspicious for ages, but just recently I've been almost certain – it's just that I thought you didn't want to talk about it . . .'

'I didn't, at first, but now it's got so bad I really can't think of anything else. I've become obsessed. I can't sleep properly, because now I'm really sure. Absolutely.'

'You are?'

'One hundred per cent certain,' said Viola.

I felt a huge surge of relief wash over me. Viola was on my side. Obviously, she had been watching Vlad for the same reasons as me, and putting two and two together. Clearly something had happened today, maybe at the library, which had confirmed her suspicions. She too had realised that Vlad was up to no good. Now she'd be able to help Callum and me trap him.

'So what made you change your mind? I mean you really liked him,' I said.

Viola looked startled.

'Change my mind? Oh, I see, you mean from just really liking someone to being totally in love. I think it was —'

'LOVE!'

'Yes, of course love. Isn't that what we've just been talking about? Oh, please, please don't say you wanted to tell me it's just a schoolgirl crush. You didn't bring me up here to talk me out of it?'

'But, but, you can't be in love with Vlad, he's . . . you're . . . too young.'

'Too young? I thought you were a writer. I'll be thirteen in November. The same age as Juliet. Was she too young to love Romeo?'

And Viola hurled herself on to my bed sobbing.

We never have any tissues so I trailed to the loo for loo paper and caught sight of a worried Candice hopping from foot to foot in the hall. The sobbing was rather loud. I went back to sit miserably beside the weeping Viola, cursing myself for being such an idiot.

'Sorry,' was all I could say. But her sobs slowly subsided.

'Oh, but it's all hopeless, hopeless, hopeless,' she moaned. 'He'll never love me! His mind's on higher things. All he thinks about is his mission to change the world.'

'No, no, he's not good enough for you. Really he's not . . . He's . . .' But I bit my tongue. I knew that if I said what I really thought of Vlad I'd lose Viola for ever. Like when someone's moaning about their mum and you join in, saying she is a bit of a bat, and they turn on you and defend their family like a tiger. But I was nearly too late.

'Not good enough? You don't still think he's a bad person do you? You know he didn't push you in front of that lorry. I told you. I asked him about it! He pushed you out of the way of a lorry! He probably saved your life! He said you had your "head in sky".' Viola grinned to herself. 'He has such a dear, quaint way of talking.'

'Yes. I know,' I said. I'd heard that he had told Viola that. I didn't believe him, but obviously she did.

Love is stronger than friendship.

'To think that I thought you understood,' continued Viola. 'I thought you were going to be so pleased for me but now I see you only wanted to talk me out of it, just like a grown up! But I'm so happy, don't you see? I've never been happier. And I'm so sad. I've never been sadder. And I don't know which is best, the happy bit or the sad bit.'

We sat in silence for a while, contemplating the mystery

of love. I felt a shivery pang, wondering if I would ever feel like Viola did, or whether I would always be an observer, on the outside.

Minutes later, Candice swept into the room in a rash display of domesticity, thinking crumpets might cheer us up. Like so much that is ordinary and comforting, crumpets with too much butter and plum jam did, in fact, have a heartening effect and I told Viola that Shakespeare had said something about women having to be 'patient on a monument smiling at grief.' Viola gave me a watery smile and said, yes, patience was the answer.

'Maybe, when Vlad's done his work, you know, achieved his mission . . . he'll suddenly remember me. Even if it's forty years from now. I'll still be here, waiting for him . . .' She paused, obviously thinking that forty years was a bit long, even for young love. Especially for young love.

'Do you think, if I am patient on a monument, that he will ever notice me?'

'I don't think it's to do with you. I don't think he's into girls, that's all. Not many boys of twelve are.'

'Tobylerone is! And anyway, Vlad looks so much older. I sometimes wonder if there's a mystery to him, like his parents faked his birth certificate to smuggle him out of the country . . .'

'Yes, I've been wondering about that myself.'

'But,' Viola continued dreamily, 'if he's not into girls

now, he will be next year, or the year after that, or the year after that. Maybe when he's sorted out his mission. I can wait.'

'What exactly is this mission of Vlad's – to change the world?' I asked in what I hoped was an interested-yet-casual tone.

'Oh, it's a huge secret. He won't go into any detail. But I know, I just know, that it's something very special and good and wonderful,' she sighed.

I wanted it to be, I really did.

But at least I knew that now I had to save Viola from Vlad's clutches. Still no text from Callum so, after Viola had drooped off home, I e-mailed Aunt Laura.

Dear Aunt Laura,
Emergency help, please. My best friend Viola says she is in love. But she's only twelve!! Please don't say Juliet was only thirteen because it was different in Shakespeare's time as everyone was dead by the time they were your age (no offence) so they had to make hay while the sun shone. But I am very worried, because the object of Viola's affections will only break her heart and ruin her young life and leave her wrecked on the shores of love. This

Vladimir she's in love with is the very same Vladimir I was worried about before. You can't be surprised by that, as there are not many Vladimirs in Falmer North, but I am beginning to get proof that he is really and truly a Bad Guy. He might even be a terrorist!

Should I tell her how awful he really is?

Please tell me Viola is just having a crush and that she will get over it. She says she's never been so happy - or so sad!

Love to the Three Bees and Joan and Joan.

And loads to you.

Cordelia xxxx

I spent the rest of the evening checking my e-mail and texting Callum every five minutes.

Finally I just put it very bluntly.

HELP, *Viola in love with Vlad*.

He rang soon after, sounding miserable.

'You think she really loves him?'

'Sounds like it.'

'Why do women always go for the bad guy?'

'They don't always.'

'We've got to save her. We've got to follow him every minute. Never let him out of our sight until we've proved he's up to no good.'

'Yeah. We've got to get into his flat somehow.'

'Ludmilla the wicked witch and her cats. I'll work it out.'

Next morning, there was an e-mail from Aunt Laura.

Darling Cordy,

It's two a.m. so a bit late to ring you. I've been in A & E again because of the mad triplets . . .

Twelve is on the young side to be in love, but it's hardly unusual to think you are at that age. I did, myself. It was the milkman's son, Eddie, whose leather jacket and Elvis Presley quiff were the coolest thing imaginable back then, hundreds of years ago. I still wouldn't call my passion for Eddie a crush, even now. I would call it 'first love'.

You will do absolutely the right thing if you take Viola seriously as she sounds in a rather fragile state and needs her friends!! Whatever you do, don't tell her what you think of

Vladimir – remember Romeo was not a suitable boy either as far as Juliet's family were concerned!!

Please, though, don't let your imagination run away with you darling. Has it occurred to you that he may be a perfectly normal boy? Be very careful of accusing someone without evidence!! I seem to think you may have done something similar before? Remember Viola's father, wrongly imprisoned!

Could you, do you think, be a little jealous of Viola caring for him? I remember going mad when my best friend developed a crush on a teacher. And as you'll notice, I still belittle her feelings forty years on by calling it a crush?

The most important thing is to hold on to your friendship with Viola and to pour your marvellous imagination into your writing, which is where it truly belongs.

Did you get the sparkly socks I sent?

A & E was ghastly. Saturday night

and lots of youths with bits of broken
bottles sticking out of them. Was
there because Bertie ate some knitting. The doc says it should pass
through naturally unless it tangles.
Other two Bees as well as can be
expected – I've only got them for two
more days and then I can get down to
some serious writing. Maybe a *Terrible
Triplets* series, based on them.

Lots and oodles of love and keep
writing!

Auntie Lolly xxxx xxxx

Knitting. Is there anything the three Bees won't eat? And
curses – I never thanked her for the socks. They're too
small anyway and have sparkly pink hearts on. Laura still
thinks I am six sometimes – or maybe that's how she
writes to everyone, all those exclamation marks. She
puts too many in her books, too. If I was her editor I'd
take them out. Still, maybe she is right . . . Could I just
be jealous? Am I imagining all this stuff about Vlad? Is
my Bond book going to my head?

The Girl with the Golden Pun (ctd)

Every second that ticked by as she stood at the casino bar seemed to Bond to be bringing humanity closer to its destruction. She slipped a hundred dollar bill into the waistband of the cute barman's trousers.

'Ms Aurelia Goldfumble, where can I find her tonight?'

The waiter recoiled as though he had been bitten by a serpent. Just my luck, thought Bond, who was used to men falling at her feet and obeying her every whim. This is the one man in Miami who does not respond to my charms . . .

At that very moment, the revolving doors of the casino swung open and a tall, towering figure strode in. Her bikini was of golden velvet, simple yet with the touch of splendour that only a dozen couturiers in the world can achieve. She wore golden chains around her long neck and muscular arms, and a tall, towering golden turban studded with precious gems on top of her tall, towering head while her enormous feet teetered precariously on tall, towering golden stilettos. In her arms purred a marmalade cat with a golden collar (That must be Zanzibar, the robotic Trojan cat, thought Bond), and surrounding her on every side was an army of magnificent young men, naked except for their golden boxer shorts. But it wasn't their absence of clothes, or even their astounding six packs, slender hips and rippling biceps that stopped Bond in her tracks.

'They're painted gold! All over!' she hissed.

'Yes,' whispered the barman. 'And soon they will die of blood poisoning because of it. Then she will get some more . . .'

'Is that why you recoiled from me as if I were a serpent at the mention of her name?' Bond whispered back, never taking her eyes from the tall, towering figure of Aurelia Goldflinger who was now approaching the gaming tables.

'Of course,' said the waiter. 'No young man is safe from her.'

But before Bond had time to reply, she felt a violent blow on the back of her head and knew no more . . .

Laura Hunt's Top Tips for Budding Writers:
Think of different forms your story might
take. How about writing your story as a
series of letters or e-mails, or even a
newspaper report?

Dear Z,
Am stuck hanging by my teeth over a vat of boiling gold.
Any tips?
Yours, Bond (Jane Bond)

Dear Bond,
Amazing. How are you writing to me then?
Are you free yet?
Yours, Z

Dear Z,
No. I fell in and knew no more.
Yours, Bond (Jane Bond)

Dear Bond,
How are you writing to me then?
Yours, Z

(And so on . . .)

Chapter Four

The next week confirmed my worst fears. Callum and I
tracked Vlad for four days after school. This was good of
Callum as he is supposed to do six hours of homework a
day at his fancy school, but now he seems as keen as I
am to save innocent Viola from the vampire . . .

What we have discovered is that, apart from going to
the library (Callum followed him inside, as Vlad doesn't

know him, and reported back that all he took out was chemistry stuff), Vlad is fascinated by water. In just one week he visited the scummy pond in the park, the weedy river full of plastic bags and beer cans at the edge of town and the outside swimming pool. And he took samples of each one. On Wednesday we caught him in a ruthless criminal act of trespass. He sneaked a look up and down the street and then vaulted over a fence into number 43! I know they have a fishpond . . . And he came out with his school bag bulging. We were lurking behind a car, but honestly I don't think he'd notice me if I walked right up to him and asked what he's doing. He's always muttering into a mobile, as though he's communicating with evil allies . . .

'Do you think he nicked the fish? Hope so, because then, if we can't prove he's a poisoner, at least we can prove he's a thief!'

Callum was all for rugby tackling Vlad in the street and ripping open his bag there and then, but I held him back.

'If he didn't nick anything we'll look stupid. If he did, we'll find out soon enough.'

We waited a few minutes and then knocked at number 43.

'We're doing a water survey, you know, because of the drinking water problem, and we wondered how your fish are?'

The bloke who answered the door looked like a fish himself, his eyes bulged bulbously and his skin shone with a fishy sheen and erupted in scaly nodules all over his cheeks. He flapped a fin at us and said the fish were fine as far as he knew and no, he was not going to his pond to check them for a 'kiddies' water survey.

'Well, if any, um, get ill, or disappear, do let me know,' I said to the closing door.

On Friday evening, we spotted the small, hooded figure again, lurking outside Vlad's house. When he came out, the figure darted behind a tree, then, as Callum and I watched from behind a car, it started shadowing Vlad down the road.

'Am I imagining it? Or is that little bloke following him too?' I clutched Callum's arm.

'Looks like it,' he said. 'Maybe someone else is on to him. A rival team of spies.'

When we turned the next corner in pursuit of Vlad, though, the figure had vanished.

'Maybe it's Death,' Callum said gloomily. 'Like in that film *The Seventh Seal*.'

'Is it about seven seals?' I asked. I'm a sucker for animal films.

'Yeah,' Callum said. 'Death picks them off and eats them, one by one.'

That night I dreamed I was pursued by angry seals in hoodies, which turned into the banshees. We've only got a week to nail Vlad before the trip to Norfolk, and I was now getting frightened at the thought of Vlad coming on the trip at all.

'He might try something on with Viola and take advantage

of her youth and innocence and you won't be there to help,' I told Callum the next day.

'I won't be there to help,' echoed Callum, his ears waving sadly. 'We're not getting anywhere. Fast.'

So Callum and I decided to kidnap one of Ludmilla's cats. In all the time we'd been spying on Vlad we hadn't seen anything of the wicked witch or her cats.

'Maybe she never lets them out.'

''Course she does; we'll get over the back fence and look for a cat flap.'

We armed ourselves with a bowl of Chat Supreme and a pillowcase to put the poor cat in and clambered over the rickety fence at the end of Vlad's garden to make ourselves uncomfortable among the briars and stingers. We gazed up at the big dilapidated old house, five floors of it, that must have been divided into flats about a hundred years ago when some old Victorian ran out of money. There was a cat flap on the ground floor but half an hour's prickly crouching led nowhere. We were about to give up when the back door opened and a stream of cats snaked out into the garden like a furry scarf. I've never seen Callum move so fast. He was out from behind the bushes, rugby tackling the nearest mog and hauling it back under the bushes quicker than you could say 'catnap'. Our victim, a hideous ginger thing, began wailing, hissing and spitting all at once, but luckily shut up as soon as it saw the Chat Supreme and gobbled away as though it hadn't eaten for days.

'Probably never gets a look in, with all those others,' said Callum tenderly, although it was the ugliest cat I've ever seen. Very long with a tiny head, like a snake, and bright yellow eyes.

'It's almost bald!' I exclaimed. 'D'you think she shaves it?'

'Shhh, she's coming out.'

We froze behind the bushes. And sure enough the wicked witch appeared for a moment bellowing at the cats to come back in.

'Hope she doesn't count them, let's get out of here, quick.'

We clambered back over the fence, carrying the poor cat in the pillowcase and ran round to the nearest climbable tree, up the road.

Callum got up the tree and I passed him the pillow-case. He hung on to the cat's hind legs and dangled it out of the tree – so he was hidden, but the cat looked like it was trapped. He did it very gently and the cat was so full of Chat Supreme that the bald snaky feline purred a bit and then fell asleep, upside down. Cats can do stuff like that.

'Now go and fetch her quickly! I don't think I can keep this up for long!'

I scampered off and banged on Ludmilla's door. Glancing back I was relieved to see there was a clear view of the dangling cat.

Ludmilla's door opened, just a fraction, and a tiny black eye gleamed fiercely out of the gloom behind the security chain.

'Yessss?' creaked her old voice.

'Your cat! I think it's one of your cats! It's stuck in a tree,' I gasped. Ludmilla wrenched back the chain and thrust her head out.

'Ivanov! My precious!' she wailed, like Gollum. 'My precious Ivanov. Where is he?'

Goodness me, either she'd noticed baldy cat had gone already or she could recognise his purr. Either way this was a true cat lover.

I pointed to the tree.

'But don't worry,' I shouted, so Callum could hear me. 'My friend is rescuing it.'

Ludmilla squinted up at the tree and sure enough Callum's face bobbed into sight on cue, clutching the snoozing Ivanov. I could see he was trying to waggle Ivanov's paws to make him look distressed.

'Oh thank you, thank you,' said Ludmilla. 'Ivanov is the grandfather of all cats.'

Minutes later, a scratched and breathless Callum arrived, clutching a now spitting and hissing Ivanov – who leapt gratefully on to Ludmilla and immediately started purring again, looking almost cute, like a baby reunited with its mother.

'Come in, come in,' said the wicked witch.

As little as two years ago I'd have been terrified of walking over that spooky threshold, but of course Ludmilla now looked just like any normal old woman and although a flat full of fifty cats smells of, well, cat, it was actually quite cosy inside. And, I was thinking, it must have exactly the same layout as Vlad's flat two floors up. I noticed Russian-looking stuff everywhere, little wooden dolls, wooden icons, books, and wondered again whether Ludmilla and Vlad might be in league.

She bustled about finding us a box of mouldy chocolate biscuits and then poured us two tiny glasses of water.

'Cheers, I thank you,' she said, taking one herself.

As I raised it to my mouth I realised it wasn't water at all. It smelled like the stuff Howard uses to oil hinges. I caught Callum's eye.

'Cheers!' he said, clinking his glass hard against Ludmilla's and winking at me.

Aha!! He was remembering that bit I'd told him I was going to write in Jane Bond, about how the Vikings clash their tankards together to check they aren't poisoned.

But Ludmilla drank happily, even though some drops from Callum's glass must have gone into her own, so I reckoned she was innocent and downed mine in one gulp. Almost immediately, I felt extremely warm and slightly fuzzy. Help! Was mine drugged after all?

'Best Russian vodka for honoured guests!' said Ludmilla happily, smacking her lips.

I'd be dead meat if Candice knew we were kidnapping cats and drinking vodka.

'It must have been frightening here with that explosion,' I said. 'Do you think it was really gas?'

'Yesss, yesss, landlord here is terrible, never checks appliances. Is hard for old woman but worse for families above. Lucky no one in top flat.'

'Do you know the people on the third floor?' I tried to sound casual. 'The boy's in my class at school. He seems very nice.'

'Oh, they are delightful Russian people. So wonderful to speak my own language to someone. My goodness, I almost forgot,' Ludmilla said, peering at her watch. 'They've got a little new kitten that isn't very well. I said I'd see how it was while they're out. You two could come up with me? So many locks, I have such difficulty.'

So many locks, eh? Aha! Extra security!

Much too eagerly, Callum and I said, Yes! We'd love to help!

'Such sweet children! So kind! Not like those horrid little boys and girls who call me a wicked witch!' she muttered, leading us out of her flat into the stairwell.

Callum's ears flapped slowly under his hair. He's trying to grow it to disguise his ears, but I'm not sure it helps – looks like two monsters trapped in a tent.

Eagerly, we peered up the staircase that spiralled gloomily towards the dark panelled hallway above. Ludmilla started up the creaky old stairs, sighing at each step. It was all we could do not to bound up ahead of her.

'Have they gone away for the weekend?' I asked, worried Vlad might return at any moment.

'No no, back late this evening. But very kind family. Worried kitten will be lonely. They say to me, "Ludmilla, you know cats, you keep eye on her." But is sad, they have to return to Russia soon and then, what becomes of Kitty?'

My heart beat faster – would Vlad vanish before I'd proved his guilt? 'When are they going back to Russia?'

'Who knows? Soon. Who knows?'

Ludmilla was fiddling with a vast old-fashioned key ring and it seemed an age before she had mastered all three locks, until finally the huge old wooden door swung open. The dim naked lightbulb revealed a cavernous panelled hall lined with forbidding doors all of the same dark wood. I shivered.

A tiny ball of fluff was shivering, too, on the mat, so Ludmilla scooped her up and made little mewing sounds in her ear. Callum said he needed the loo and signalled for me to keep Ludmilla and Kitty occupied while he snooped about. I produced the spare tin of Chat Supreme that I'd kept in case we needed more for the great Cat Kidnap. Ludmilla didn't seem at all surprised that I should be carrying a tin of cat food around with me.

'This'll cheer her up, it's like cat's caviare,' I said as Ludmilla and I hunted in the dark little kitchen for a tin opener until Callum reappeared in the doorway, eyes aflame, gesturing frantically towards a room next to the bathroom.

'Oooh, I need the loo too, must've been that vodka,' I said, although I needn't have bothered as Ludmilla was happily administering to Kitty.

'Take some photos,' hissed Callum. 'My battery's run out.'

I entered the room, mobile at the ready. It seemed that someone slept here, because there was an unmade bed, but in every other respect it was like a miniature version of the school science labs, crammed higgledy-piggledy with hundreds of potions, test tubes, measuring flasks, Bunsen burners and various dangerous looking substances. The walls were papered with diagrams, formulae and maps. In the middle was a large box, labelled *Danger* with a skull and crossbones on it, like those symbols you see on electric pylons. I took about fifty snaps, one ear listening out for Callum, who was trying to engage Ludmilla in a complicated discussion, pretending he thought there was something weird about Kitty's paws. I snapped away until my battery ran out, then we tried to disentangle ourselves from Ludmilla as quickly as we could, ignoring her plaintive invitations to come again soon and asking how she could repay us for saving Ivanov.

Just as we left, I begged her not to say anything to Vlad's family about our visit.

'Why not? You have been so kind.'

'I think he would be embarrassed to think someone from his school had seen his flat. He's very shy.'

'I understand. I was the same. Is fine to be alone when you are young. Now, I would love it if people came to see me.'

'So you won't tell?'

'I won't tell.'

Without thinking, I gave her a hug. It was like hugging a skeleton. But a friendly one.

'She probably spends all her pension on cat food,' I said to Callum, silently vowing to buy her a tin or two at Christmas.

We spent a frustrating hour going through the fuzzy pictures on Callum's laptop, looking for further clues and stuff to show what Vlad was up to.

'Did you see that kitten's paws?' asked Callum.

'No. Why?'

'They had six toes.'

'Really? I thought you were just trying to distract Ludmilla, going on about its feet.'

'Probably another of Vlad's experiments. Mutations . . .' mused Callum, before springing into action at the next picture to come up on the screen.

'Phew, 0007, take a look at this . . . It's the playground! And he's circled the pond!' Sure enough, on the walls of the 'laboratory' there were two maps of the park, with a telltale felt-pen ring around the polluted pond!

'And look, this one, blow it up more! See? It's Ms Parker's new "wildlife garden" in Falmer North playground! He's circled the pond there, too.'

'But look, this one's even scarier,' said Callum, homing in on a huge fuzzy photo.

'Why?'

'It's the garden at Buckingham Palace! With a huge X on the lake . . .'

'He's testing out a deadly poison on a kids' playground,' I hissed. 'He's checking out ponds and water all over the place to work out the best poisons! He's going to go after Falmer North's wildlife garden, and then the Queen!'

'Wait a minute, him being interested in formulae and test tubes and maps and all that doesn't make him a Bad Guy,' Callum objected. 'I mean, he's a boy – I'm interested in stuff like that too.'

'You are?' I asked.

'We'll just have to draw him deeper into the net to get him to reveal himself,' Callum announced dramatically. 'We have to convince him we understand what his mission is.'

'We do?' I said.

'You'll have to really talk to him, tell him you understand and that you'll do anything for him to help The Cause.'

'I will?' I said, feeling a little like I was stuck in a revolving door.

'We have to make sacrifices for Queen and Country. The lives of two little people don't amount to a hill of beans in this crazy world . . .' Callum said.

'Oh, stop being a movie nerd, you're always . . . WHAT?!' I froze. I had been vaguely looking at the screen while we were talking, magnifying sections of the pictures we hadn't looked at closely. Pinned next to the map of Buckingham Palace was a photo of – me!

'Are you sure?' Callum peered at the picture, once I'd made it clear what I was ogling at.

''Course I'm sure! It's very fuzzy, it looks as if it's been cut out from a tiny picture . . . but it is me! I'm certain of it!'

'He must know you're suspicious of him. Why else would he have your photo on his wall?'

A cold shiver crept over me. Had Vlad been trying to push me under the lorry after all? I'd begun to believe Viola's version but now I was doubting again.

'Well, maybe you can turn this to your advantage,' said Callum. 'Is there a way of getting Vlad on his own?'

''Course there is. The field trip to Norfolk,' I said

decisively. 'But I'm worried, Cal. If he's already suspicious of me, why would he confide in me? And how do I keep him from getting his clutches on Viola?'

'That's the most important thing of all. Apart from him bumping you off, of course,' Callum added quickly. 'But if he's suspicious of you – if he's noticed you keeping an eye on him – then maybe that's exactly what we need. You have to tell him you've been watching him for a while, that you're writing a book, that you want to know his secret, because, like him, you want to change the world too. Then he's bound to let something slip and then he's in the bag. Once you've got even a shred of hard evidence then we can call in the cops, and one look at his bedroom laboratory will convince them of the rest. So we'll save Viola! And, erm, the Queen and so on.'

There were only two more days till the field trip and nothing unusual happened, except, one night, I spotted the hooded figure again, beside the playground pool. Vlad was silhouetted against his window and the figure was staring up at him from behind a bush, but I couldn't see any communication going on between them. Were they making secret signs, or using high pitched bat squeaks, inaudible to the human ear?

When Vlad drew his curtains, the figure sort of drooped and seconds later it had vanished.

Laura Hunt's Top Tips for Budding Writers:
You can't write well without reading a lot.
Read everything - as much as you can.

Excellent. It is noon on Saturday and today I have read:

> *1) The back of the shampoo bottle.*
> *2) The back of the conditioner bottle.*
> *3) The back of the two-in-one shampoo*
> *and conditioner bottle.*
> *4) An article in Mizz Frizz magazine about how to care*
> *for your hair.*

Now I have so much information about hair products that I can't decide which to use. But there is not single piece of advice for hair that looks like a mushroom.

The Girl with the Golden Pun (ctd)

Bond woke, gasping for breath as she tried to keep her head above water, entrapped in the tentacles of some savage beast. Help! she thought. I am in a tank full of octopuses! Or is it octopi?

As the tentacles tightened round her throat, threatening to silence her husky tonsils forever, she reached into the secret pocket of her now sodden golden leather trouser suit and drew out a small, but perfectly formed, underwater explosive.

'I never travel without one,' Z had told her before she left. She pressed the small aluminium lever and a blinding explosion blew her and the six tentacled beasts (two of which were in fact giant squid) out of the water. The sea beasts flailed on the floor of the damp cave on to which they had been flung and Bond fainted with shock and once again knew no more.

She awoke with a fearsome headache. She was in a dim, candlelit dungeon, the air thick with smoke! They were burning her alive! She made to get up, but found herself bound by extremely slender, but exceptionally strong, golden chains.

'You cannot escape. You can either tell me everything you know, in which case you can accompany my mistress on her mission to create a super race among the stars, or you can die a long slow death at the hands of a rusty saw.'

Bond immediately recognised Dr Midas, Aurelia Goldbangle's one-legged, steel-toothed, metal-rimmed bowler-hatted, bayonet-booted, ruthless sidekick and hired assassin. It must be Dr Midas, she thought, unless there were other one-legged, steel-toothed, metal-rimmed bowler-hatted, bayonet-booted ruthless sidekicks and hired assassins in the vicinity.

'Tell me, which reality TV show did they get you out of?' she spat at him.

'Don't make it tougher on yourself, Miss Bond!' snarled Midas, slapping her across the face. 'My orders are to kill you. How I do it is my business, but I assure you it'll be slow and agonising. But first you must kiss my feet!'

'I think you mean, foot,' said Bond, before recoiling under the stab of Midas's bayonetted boot.

'OK, I get the point,' said Bond, her full pouting lips tightening with pain. 'But your methods are a trifle brutish. That's the trouble with the underworld these days. Nobody takes the time to do a lengthy, sinister interrogation. It's a lost art.'

Midas responded with another bayonet stab, this time to Bond's right thigh.

The sharp agony ran through her body in a twinkling and she convulsed with pain and, once again, knew no more.

Laura Hunt's Top Tips for Budding Writers:
Is your character in a tricky situation and you don't know how to get him or her out of it? Think what YOU would do in the same situation and then ask yourself if your character is like you or not and what would they do differently.

This might be helpful if I am ever in a vat of octopuses.

Chapter Five

Ever been seriously embarrassed by your parents? Like
BOTH parents coming to see you off for a four day school
trip? To Norfolk? As if you are off backpacking round the
world and they're not going to see you for a year? And
then checking the tyres on the coach?

It's pretty hard to imagine anything worse than your
mum prodding all the tyres and asking if the pressure is
OK – at least Howard had the decency to shuffle around
looking embarrassed and pretending to help Mr Frost
stow all the luggage into the bottom of the coach.
Candice capped it all by warbling in her loudest, poshest
voice, 'Have you got your hotty, darling? It'll be freezing

in Norfolk and those youth hostels are absolutely dismal.'

'Mum!' I hissed 'It's June!' She looked startled and then, to give her her due, I could see she realised that I was calling her mum because no one else calls their mum Candice. So she gave me a hug and whispered 'Sorry. Have fun,' and I suddenly thought I was going to be horribly homesick.

OK, I admit it: I am young and skinny, so I do feel the cold and I do have a hot water bottle most of the year. But do I want the whole school to know that?

'Was that your mum checking out the tyres?'

'And asking if you needed your POTTY?'

Potty was even worse than hotty.

The banshees subsided into a chant that managed to rhyme spotty, botty, grotty and snotty before giving up and burying their snouts in a trough of crisps.

Parky and Frosty gave us a little talk about Health and Safety issues, telling us not to be tempted to go swimming. Apparently, 'whilst the water may look very appealing . . .' (derisive hoots from banshees about dipping their toes in the freezing English sea) '. . . it is always very cold and the shock can kill. There are underwater hazards such as weeds, rapid currents and poisonous blue-green algae.'

Vlad was scribbling notes furiously, obviously wondering if he could get hold of some of this algae to add to his poison collection.

'The Norfolk Broads is a magnificent national park of lowland and water-based protected areas, linked together by miles of river,' droned Frosty, reading from a tour guide while the driver checked the seat belts and emergency exits under Candice's beady eye.

'We'll be driving through beautiful open countryside and passing charming villages with medieval churches and we may get to see Norwich Cathedral which has the second highest spire and largest monastic cloisters in England!' Frosty could see he was losing us. 'And guess who's buried there?' He peered round with a wicked gleam in his eye.

'My granny,' said Little Lucy, her bottom lip trembling.

'He means someone famous, dumbo,' said Mathadi and Lucy burst into tears.

'Your granny is in good company, Lucy. Archbishop Matthew Parker is buried in Norwich. He was always checking up on his clergymen, so people think he was the original Nosy Parker!' said Frosty, with a sly look at Ms Parker.

Everybody giggled. 'No relation,' she said. 'Into the coach quick sharp.'

I made sure I bagged the seat next to Viola on the coach, partly because she's getting friendlier with more people these days but mainly because I didn't want to have to watch her asking Vlad to sit next to her and being refused. It's painful to see her trying to get his attention.

He's so rude. Just sits with his nose in a book. Bit like me, but for different reasons.

Sure enough, Vlad sat near the back of the coach on his own, reading *Chemical Journeys*.

'I worry about him, always on his own. He must be so lonely,' said Viola tenderly.

'He likes it,' I said firmly. I could punch her sometimes.

Vlad was far from lonely. Jolene, Zandra and the rest of the banshees kept offering him crisps and toffees, and snobby Sasha found about forty million reasons to traipse up and down the coach past him and drop things into his lap. She eventually managed to trip up accidentally-on-purpose and drop herself into his lap, but it all made no difference to Vlad, who read on, robotically.

'You were right. At least he doesn't seem interested in anyone else,' sighed Viola, settling down to read I *Capture the Castle*. 'You know, this is the sort of book I'd like to write,' she said. 'It's so dreamy, so funny, so romantic. It's all about how young people see things so much more clearly than old people. I'm just like Cassandra. I think you could write something like this yourself.'

'Fat chance,' I said. My writing was a sore point just at that moment. I couldn't see how to get Jane Bond away from Dr Midas's bayonetted boot. And I still hadn't even decided what to call my villain . . .

'Oh, but you could, you know. You're going to be a much better writer than your Aunt Laura.'

'Shut up, will you?' Viola knows I still haven't told anyone else at school that the fabulous Laura Hunt is my aunt. My life wouldn't be worth living for autograph hunters. But I wanted to defend Aunt Laura just the same. 'I thought you loved her books!'

'I did. I still do, but maybe I'm growing out of them, just a bit . . .' Viola gazed out at the drizzle as the coach bumped along past fields of depressed-looking cows and shivering sheep.

At least I didn't have to be concerned about Vlad trying to get his evil clutches on Viola. One worry to cross off my list. I had a sudden desire to end her passion once and for all by telling her what Callum and I had seen in his room, but a little voice whispered in my ear. The voice was Aunt Laura's. 'Remember Romeo was not a suitable boy either, as far as Juliet's family were concerned . . . Has it occurred to you he may be a perfectly normal boy?' It was enough to shut me up. I sat back and dozed.

Norfolk was flat and rainy. I expect it can be flat and windy or flat and sunny or even flat and snowy, but rain and mud was what we got.

'This is rubbish weather, Miss. You got it wrong about global warming,' said Tobylerone cheerfully, as he threw everyone's bags out of the hold of the coach and into a pond. Well, a big puddle.

'Be careful, Toby, you'll ruin our lovely ballgowns,' hooted the banshees.

Nosy Parker made a little speech about respecting each other's property and was at pains to point out that global warming didn't just mean beaches and Cornettos all year. She looked pointedly at Jolene as she said this but Jolene was screaming at Toby for getting mud on her new wellies.

She has got bonkers high-heeled welly boots! With hearts on!

'Global warming can give rise to all sorts of extreme weather conditions,' shouted Ms Parker above the howling gale. 'Storms, hurricanes, even earthquakes.'

Youth hostels have obviously improved since Candice's day – it was cosy with nice little bunk beds, four to a room.

Viola and I were in with Mathadi, who's noisy and fun, and Lucy, who, as well as looking about six, had brought a bag that seemed to be full of nothing but soft toys.

'Didn't you bring any pyjamas?' I asked. Tears sprang to her eyes, so I lent her my spare pair and, even though I'm small, she looked like a pea in a sack. She cheered up immediately and insisted we had a midnight feast so we all spent the first evening nicking as much as we could from supper then sitting up watching the wild rain on the wild sea, telling ghost stories and eating cold sausages. Bliss. Except Lucy started crying again when Mathadi told a story about a youth hostel ghost roaming the country looking for someone called Little Lucy, who it needed to eat.

'It's quite a romantic place, isn't it?' whispered Viola as I drifted off to sleep. I didn't worry that she'd try tippy-toeing along to the boys' rooms because I knew that:

a) Vlad would barricade himself in, and

b) Mr Frost had told us anyone up after lights out would be shot on sight, no questions asked.

Next morning, we all had to drag ourselves out of bed at seven and stuff ourselves with eggs and sausages before trudging around a bird sanctuary with our sketch books. As far as I could see, the birds had all very sensibly taken sanctuary elsewhere on account of the freezing wind and howling gale, although lots of kids and Ms Parker seemed to spot thousands of them.

At lunch (a freezing picnic in the shelter of Norfolk's only tree) we shared our 'discoveries'. Mathadi had seen a lesser-spotted willow warbler, or something that is 'fantastically rare on our shores' as Ms P declared.

'I've seen corn buntings, a godwit and a gorgeous flock of yellow wagtails, with bright yellow under bits,' she enthused, to muffled giggles. 'And poor little Lucy was scared by a booming bittern, weren't you, Lucy?'

'Yeth,' lisped Lucy, who was enjoying being a weed. 'AND I saw a huge scary dragonfly called a Norfolk Hawker.'

Lucy's drawing of the Norfolk Hawker was actually

quite scary, and Frosty said that although it was a harmless thing, Lucy had captured it 'very well indeed'. Lucy blushed and simpered. She had adopted Viola and me as big sisters and was beginning to get on my nerves.

Eric Cubicle hadn't seen anything so he'd invented a bird with four wings, which he'd drawn with lots of technical measurements and arcs and protractors so that it looked like an aeroplane. 'It can fly for ever, cos it uses the spare wings when the first pair get tired, which is after it has flown 96.347 kilometres,' he explained. I wonder if he takes a ruler to bed to see how long he sleeps?

'Soon we will have birds like those with, what you say, genetic engineering,' said Vlad. He should know – look at his kitten.

'Yeah, and four-legged chickens,' said Tobylerone. 'So there's more of 'em to eat. I reckon the burger bars are doing that, building a steak instead of growing a whole cow.'

'Your thinking is woolly, but on the right lines, Toby,' said Mr Frost. 'We must ask ourselves, do we want, or need, such things? Naturally we need food that is energy efficient to produce, but suppose these new inventions give rise to mutated animals and even people. Would we like that?'

'Yeah, like that mouse with an ear growing on its back. That was evil,' said Toby.

'Not evil – science,' said Vlad darkly.

'Yeah, I think it's great,' said Eric. 'We could have loads of spare parts and iPods instead of kidneys. And we could fly instead of drive, which would be good for the environment, wouldn't it, Mr Frost?'

'But suppose we unleash deadly chemicals into the environment and we can't find a way to neutralise them?' said Ms Parker.

'Exactly,' whispered Vlad. He was grinning to himself and nodding. I thought of the cat's paws. Was there no end to his evil?

But I still couldn't see a way to get him on his own and talk to him without Viola being around.

Poor old Viola sorted out the problem for me by putting her foot in a cattle grid on the way back and twisting her ankle so badly she had to be carried the rest of the way to the youth hostel by Mr Frost and Tobylerone. There we found Jolene and Zandra, lying wrapped up in blankets on sofas in the common room, suffering from nervous exhaustion as a result of having to carry a backpack and a biro.

'No one told us how dangerous the countryside was,' said Zandra. 'It's all nettles and thorns and things with horns. It's given me an allergy, Miss, really it has. My bum's come up all red and spotty. D'you want to see it?'

'And I've got welly-bootitis,' moaned Jolene. 'Wearing wellies has made my feet go mouldy. Honestly, Miss, they've gone all green and fluffy. D'you want to see?'

'No, thank you very much. You can look after Viola,' said Ms Parker briskly. 'Really,' I heard her mutter, 'some girls don't know they're born. When I was in Africa, kids walked five miles to school with bare feet and swam across crocodile-infested waters, they were so keen to get an education.'

Viola seemed quite pleased to be in the cosy common room with the banshees. I left them all gossiping about their ailments in front of the telly while I got kitted up for our next outing – to the wetlands to look at water birds and algae.

I seized my opportunity with Vlad as soon as we set off. He always hung out at the back and, with Jolene and Zandra and Viola out of the way and Lucy and Sasha sucking up to Mr Frost, no one was watching. I asked him if he was enjoying the trip and he jumped like a startled rabbit, his eyes like headlamps.

'What's up? You look like you've swallowed a golf ball. Cat got your tongue?'

'Gofe ball? Cat got my tongue?'

'Oh. It's just a way of saying you can't find the words, it's just a . . .'

'Colloquialism?' he said.

'That's right. Your English is better than you pretend, isn't it?'

'Yes. I try to keep people away. So I can think.'

'Why did you look so shocked just now?'

'Just that you spoke to me. You are the only one who never speaks to me.'

'I want to speak to you for a good reason,' I said conspiratorially. 'I think we have the same thoughts.'

'Really?'

'Yes, you see, I'm a writer, or I will be soon.'

'I knew you were clever,' he said.' The first time I saw you.'

I felt myself blush, but I wasn't going to be diverted from my plan. I knew I had to trap Vlad into sharing his Big Idea with me. I had to get him to trust me.

'I'm trying to write about a hero – a sort of revolutionary who's really, really clever. A kind of scientific genius. In fact, my inspiration for this character is you.'

It was Vlad's turn to blush. Good! He was flattered!

'Do you ever feel you understand something other people don't?' I continued.

'All the time. There is pollution everywhere,' he said despairingly. 'In the air, in the earth – but mainly in the mind. Those who understand have to stamp it out.'

'Whatever the cost,' I said, encouragingly.

'Oh, I don't mind what it costs,' agreed Vlad.

'And you have to start at the top,' I said. 'Get the leader, and all else follows.'

'I am very close to achieving this,' Vlad said mysteriously. 'You will see. It's so nice to meet someone with whom one can share these things.'

'Yes, you see, we think alike. I want to change the world too. I have plans myself. I could help you . . .'

'You'd like to help? To rid the world of this . . . poison altogether?'

'Yes! But, sometimes, things we love must be destroyed to make the world better,' I said, encouragingly.

'Exactly.' Vlad looked at the ground, his shoulders sagging.

'How are you going to achieve it? I wonder if it's anything like the ideas I have worked out for my hero? Please tell me so I can put it in my book.'

'I'd love to tell you. I'd love to share it. But would you tell anyone else? You see, things like this could get into the wrong hands . . .'

'No! It would be just our secret.'

'Just ours?' He stopped and stared at me very intensely.

'Yes, I won't tell a soul. Just you and me . . .'

His eyes shone and I felt certain he was going to reveal his plan there and then.

'Later, yes? Now is not the time,' he said and I realised I'd been so involved in our talk that I hadn't noticed the frantic gestures of Parky and Frosty, who were waving their arms about wildly to get us all into a huddle to look at some interesting twigs.

'Now, we want you in pairs for the wetlands walk,' said Frosty. 'Look after Lucy, Cordelia.'

Lucy was on the verge of tears because she had trodden on a frog.

'I think it is mortally wounded,' she sobbed. 'It will have limped off to die all alone and its little baby frogs will be waiting for it to come home and it will never come and they will starve!'

'No, no, they are little spawns, or tadpoles – they will be fine,' I said. 'Anyway, frogs don't limp, you know, they hop. And they're tough as old boots, I've heard.'

Lucy brightened slightly.

I watched Vlad, who sloped off reluctantly with Eric Cubicle, his face still shining with that odd fanatical gleam.

And there was no chance to get Vlad on his own for the rest of the trip as Viola's ankle recovered enough for her to stick to me like Velcro.

On the last night Frosty and Parker had organised a typically Spartan campfire and a sing song as a treat. Jolene and Zandra were not thrilled. They'd packed crop tops and mini-skirts for the last night party and insisted on wearing them anyway.

Snobby Sasha did her Charlotte Church impression, warbling away in Italian and Parky applauded wildly and said we had the next Pavarotti in our midst.

'But Pavarotti's huge, and a man,' said Mathadi.

'And dead,' added Tobylerone, which made Lucy cry.

Viola hobbled about, glued to my side, asking me yet again how Vlad had been while she was stuck indoors, and if he had shown any signs of missing her. Vlad actually smiled in our direction once, through the flickering flames of the camp fire and Viola made a strange squeaking sound, like a mouse on a big dipper.

'Did you see that? He smiled at me! He did, didn't he?'

'I didn't notice,' I said.

But I managed to corner Vlad for a few seconds before we all went to bed.

'Come to my house and I can show you everything,' he said.

The thought of being in that spooky block alone with him gave me goose pimples on my goose pimples.

I must have looked as scared as I felt, because Vlad said quickly, 'Or we could meet anywhere. You choose.'

'Yes, yes, somewhere secret, with no parents. Or librarians,' I added. I knew it had to be somewhere out-side, where Callum could hide easily. 'And we need water!'

'We need water! Yes! You DO understand!' said Vlad. 'Then I can demonstrate what I have learned. Let us meet at the river, by the old chestnut tree. Tomorrow?'

'I can't make tomorrow,' I said, panicking that it would be too short notice for Callum.

We agreed on Tuesday just as Viola limped into sight and turned the colour of raspberries.

Vlad took off like a rocket.

'You were talking to Vlad!' said Viola accusingly. 'What

were you saying?'

'Nothing. He just wanted to know the word for frogspawn,' I said wildly.

'Did he mention me?' she said.

'No. But I'll ask him if he likes you next time if you want.'

'Don't you dare!' she said. 'But you see what I mean about him – he is . . . wonderful, isn't he?'

'Seen worse, I suppose.'

I really wanted to share this stuff about Vlad with Viola, but I knew I shouldn't. Instead, I wrote about Jane Bond furiously into the night.

Maybe I should make Hunky Misterson a traitor, like Vlad . . .

Laura Hunt's Top Tips for Budding Writers:

When you're finishing your story, don't forget the people or things you began with. We need to know what happened to all the characters. So read your manuscript through carefully – and then read it again!

Phew, do you really have to read it twice? Seems like hard work to me. Cordelia's Lazy Writer's Tip: Don't have too many characters . . .

The Girl with the Golden Pun (ctd)

Bond woke again, this time to a soothing Mozart quartet, being played by four gold-painted naked men.

'I must have died and gone to heaven,' she murmured, before realising that another sound underlying the soft music was the whirring purring of Zanzibar, the marmalade robot cat.

'Cheers,' said an oddly vile voice. It was Aurelia Goldfangler herself, reclining on a dazzling golden chaise-longue, this time in a gold lace bikini that looked as if it had been knitted by a million elves. She handed Bond a drink – a medium sweet Martini with a slice of lime.

'I believe you like it stirred, not shaken?' she asked. 'Just to be different from your brother, James. Good thinking; we women must stick together.' And she clashed her glass savagely against Bond's.

'CHEERS! If we clink our glasses hard enough, the liquids from the two glasses will leap out and a few drops of mine will intermingle with yours whilst a few drops of yours intermingle with mine. That way, we both know that neither of us is being poisoned by the other . . . It is an old Viking custom. Good, no?'

Bond nodded coolly and knocked back the drink, her mind racing as if it was her very own battleship grey Aston Martin with its retracting chariot-style scimitar wheels, ejector seats for unwanted passengers, and bootful of starving piranhas.

'That idiot Midas was a little over-zealous,' continued Goldflinger, 'but Hunky here assures me that you are the very person to help me out.'

Goldflinger called over her shoulder.

'Take good care of Miss Bond, Hunky, dearest. See that some harm comes to her.'

Bond looked up in surprise to see that among the gold-painted men who were attending to Aurelia Goldfumbler's every whim, there was the familiar chiselled profile of – Hunky Masterson! So he was working for Goldbungler! He was a double agent! He had betrayed her!

Masking her disappointment, Bond smiled a silky smile at Goldwobbler.

'You expect me to help you?'

'No, Miss Bond, we expect you to die! Hunky here tells me you have been sent to spy on me, so naturally my dear Midas thought it necessary to eliminate you. But first, Miss Bond, I need just a little information about your famous Z.'

'If you are planning to blow us all up, then why discover anything? Z will be dead – we will all be dead.'

'You underestimate me, Miss Bond. The milk of human kindness flows in my veins. Liquid gold milk. Ah! How I love gold! I love its glitter, its brilliance, its heavenly heaviness.' Goldbungler toyed with her golden food (lemon soufflé, chicken turmeric, peach meringue with custard) watching

Bond closely as she did so. Twenty-four hours without a snack were taking their toll and Bond was weak with hunger. Aurelia Goldfangle flung a handful of yellow Smarties to her army of golden men, who jumped up and caught them neatly in their golden mouths, like so many golden retrievers.

'Naturally, Miss Bond, I would prefer not to kill everyone on the planet. We have a beautiful planet, do we not? And there are also so many gorgeous young men I have not yet met! It would be a shame to destroy them all. No, I would rather simply gain world domination, but it seems your Z is not keen to surrender all the gold to me. I thought the spectacle of you, dangling over a vat of melting gold and being slowly drowned in it, might move him to change his mind? What do you think?'

Bond felt her legs being pulled from under her and, simultaneously, an excruciating pain, as the extremely slender, but exceptionally strong, golden chain tying them together tightened and yanked her to the ceiling of the cave by her ankles. From there she dangled, swinging slowly back and forth, back and forth, like a gold leather pendulum. Below her bubbled a vast pot of molten gold. She stifled a scream. With each swing she was lowered towards it.

'Z is watching this pretty scene on his laptop, thanks to darling Hunky,' said Goldbangle. 'Look, we can see him watching you die . . .'

Bond wrenched her head around to gaze at the huge wall screen on the side of the cave. She could see Z, his head in his hands, watching her swing.

And then, to her horror, he simply turned off the screen.

'See Bond? That is how much, or should I say how very little, your paymaster cares for you. He will now be putting his next plan into action. He will be storming my base in Geneva. Little does he know that we are many thousands of miles from there and that my base is primed with a vast bomb, big enough to destroy one third of the planet. I think that will be more successful than blowing up the whole thing, don't you? Of course, the whole planet will be a nuclear wasteland for years, but my beloved boys and I will be on our rocket to a Brave New World by then and we won't let it become evil and corrupt the way this poor planet has! We will remain pure and strong! And in twenty years' time we will return to Earth. Heh! Heh! Heh!'

Bond had faced many dangers defeating the world's most evil villains, but Aurelia Goldwarbler took the biscuit.

If she could only swing a little higher, she thought, her thoughts racing even faster than her beloved Aston Martin with its scimitars and accessories, she could clasp on to the stalagmite that was hanging almost within reach. With any luck, she could wrench it off the cave's ceiling and it would plummet down and pierce Goldfangler's wicked heart. Then she could charm the golden men into releasing her. But that sort of thing only happened in books, like the ones about her brother. And, anyway, it was a stalactite she remembered because stalactites are the ones that point down . . .

The vat of molten gold was coming perilously close; soon it would scorch the ends of her slinky golden tresses. If she got out of here alive, her hairdresser would have a fit.

I must master my fear, she told herself, cursing inwardly that even in these times of terror she was forced to use the word master, because so many words were just all about men. With every ounce of her remaining strength she propelled herself to swing in a wider arc, using her using her arms to build momentum. Right . . . left . . . right . . . left. Higher and higher she swung until the stalactite was almost within her grasp. But however high she swung, the downward arc brought her closer and closer to the vile bubbling cauldron of golden doom that awaited her . . .

The golden cauldron gave off strangely familiar but nauseating fumes. Bond fought for breath, but was overcome. Once again she knew no more . . .

Laura Hunt's Top Tips for Budding Writers:

Don't know what to write about?

Why not start with a true experience: something sad or funny or embarrassing that really happened to you. Now add some new characters, a different place, dramatic events, an outrageous conclusion. Now your own true story has magically become fiction and you can do whatever you want!

Sure. It really was me hanging over that vat of boiling gold while a bomb ticked away. That was based on me getting stuck upside down on the climbing frame when the lunch bell was ringing back in primary school. So, you see, this tip does work.

Chapter Six

I called for Callum at eight p.m. on Tuesday, clutching a folder stuffed with mangled old formulae I'd printed off the internet and, in a fit of last minute inspiration, a can of fly spray, a bottle of bleach and some rat poison.

'What's that lot for?' said Callum. 'You look like a bag lady.'

'I told Vlad that I had plans too. I want him to think I'm serious about poisons and toxins.'

'If he's serious he'll have serious stuff. He won't take you seriously with that lot. The folder's good though,' he said, rifling through it quickly. 'But I'd leave out the cookie recipe.'

'Is that what it is? I thought it was for making bombs.'

'Toffee nut bombs, idiot,' said Callum.

This is the problem with Googling stuff, as teachers are always telling us. You can get the wrong end of the stick.

'Got the dictaphone?'

'Yeah – dictaphone, notebook, mobile,' Callum said confidently, patting his pockets. I hoped recording on the dictaphone – which I'd swiped from Howard – would work. A dyslexic note taker was not what I needed.

'Suppose Vlad sees you spying on us – then he'll know who you are and set his gang on you. You might be in danger for years to come. Remember that bloke the Russians poisoned with an umbrella? Or that guy who was poisoned with polonium? He was Russian too! You need a disguise.'

'Hmmm.' Callum rifled around under his bed, where he still keeps a box of old dressing-up stuff. He pulled out dusty Halloween bandages, a set of fairy wings that I'd worn when I was three and a cowboy hat. Seeing all that stuff again brought a lump to my throat.

'We could do trick or treat this year, couldn't we? We're not too big yet?' I asked hopefully.

'Look here, 0007, keep your mind on the job.'

'The hat will be good. For your ears, I mean.'

'Thanks a lot.' Callum slammed the cowboy hat hard down over his flappers. He squinted in the mirror. 'Good, but not good enough. Aha!' And he drew out a Batman mask. 'The very thing!'

So, with Callum in a long raincoat, a cowboy hat and a Batman mask, we snuck out of the house and made our way to the scuzzy old river, where it leads down to the graveyard.

'Why on earth did you choose here?' said Callum, shivering. 'And why so late?'

I'd been regretting that myself. It was already beginning to get dark.

Callum hoisted himself into the branches of the horse chestnut tree and squatted there, giving me the thumbs up.

'Sound check,' he said.

Unfortunately the dictaphone only seemed to record at virtually shouting level. He came a few branches closer and we crossed our fingers. And waited.

I sat at the foot of the tree, fingering the can of fly spray in my pocket. If Vlad tried any funny business I could use it.

At eight fifty-five, Vlad emerged through the gloom, carrying a huge box file.

'You came,' he said, with a grin of triumph.

'Yes! Here I am, Vladimir Vyshinsky!' I shouted into the tree. 'Have you brought your plans for world domi-nation with you?'

'Why are you shouting?' said Vlad.

'Am I? I have an ear infection. It's made me deaf, you'll have to speak up.' I bellowed. 'Don't worry, there's no one near by. So, VLADIMIR, have you got your plans for WORLD DOMINATION with you?'

'Everything I am doing is in here,' said Vlad, opening his file.

'You'll have to explain it all to me. WHAT IS THIS FORMULA FOR?' I yelled.

'What I plan to do is . . .'

'Speak up, Vlad! My ear is painful.'

Vlad looked round nervously. Guilt was written all over his face.

'But you know, I need to keep it secret until . . .'

'You say you need to keep it secret until what?' I bawled.

'Until I can . . .'

But, at this momentous moment, just when he was about to reveal all, Vlad was silenced by an ominous C-R-R-REAK! Followed by a more ominous C-R-R-RACK! Help! Callum had obviously shifted as close as he could but the branch couldn't hold him! I looked up in terror just in time to see a flapping masked figure, its raincoat spread like wings (very like the real Batman, if he wore a cowboy hat), swooping out of the tree above us and plummeting into the filthy river below.

Vlad grabbed me, pinning my arms to my sides so I couldn't reach the fly spray, or Callum, or anything. For a few terrible seconds I believed he was going to hurl me into the river after Callum.

'It can't be a vampire, not in the twenty-first century – don't be frightened,' he said, his voice calm and manly, although he was shaking like a leaf.

I threw him off and plunged into the murky water, desperately grasping at Callum's coat as he sank beneath the surface. Vlad plunged in too, but instead of pushing me under he grabbed at Callum's collar and together we heaved him, up to the bank. He was unbelievably heavy. And completely still.

'He's dead!' I screamed. 'It's all my fault! No! It's all your fault!' I wailed tragically, turning on Vlad. 'You killed him!'

'You know him? He is your boyfriend?' said Vlad, almost as tragically. He pulled Callum into a sitting position and walloped him on the back.

'Don't touch him! Leave him alone!' I shrieked. But a thin stream of water came from Callum's mouth and he started coughing.

'See? He is not dead,' said Vlad, looking disappointed.

'I am not dead,' agreed Callum. 'It's OK.'

'You're alive!' I squeaked, quite overcome with emotion.

'Why did you bring him to our meeting?' asked Vlad furiously. 'You think I am going to leap on you? You do not trust me?'

'Of course I don't trust you, why should I?' I turned on him indignantly. 'You're the terrorist. If you weren't plotting to poison the Queen none of this would have happened.'

'Poison what queen?' seethed Vlad.

'Don't pretend you don't know, you're plotting the downfall of society – you agreed we have to destroy the world to change it!'

'What? That was just your foolish idea for a book! I am trying to SAVE the world.'

'Aaaahhh . . .' Callum said, slowly, sitting up fully and removing his Batman mask.

'He's just a kid. What do you see in him?' said Vlad.

'It's not like that. Anyway, he's as old as you. Nearly. Or have you been lying about that, too?'

'I have not lied about anything,' said Vlad, slumping to the ground with his head in his hands. 'I trusted you. I thought . . .'

'That I would help you poison the Queen and poison little kids!'

'Cordelia,' said Callum. 'Can't you see you've got it wrong?'

And of course, I could see, almost all of it. I just felt too stupid to admit my mistake . . .

Callum had started shivering, but we needed the full picture from Vlad so we went to Joe's coffee house and Vlad told us all. Turns out his father is a distinguished Russian scientist who's in the UK, working on an important environmental pollution project.

Vlad, far from being a terrorist, has been following in his dad's footsteps by setting up a lab in his flat. With no help from his dad, who he adores and has been trying to impress, Vlad has discovered the cause of the pollution in the playground pond!

'I discovered the final link in the chain in Norfolk. It's a rare form of blue-green poisonous algae and it must have been transported by birds. It might even help us understand more about bird flu,' he said excitedly. Then, stirring his latte morosely he looked at me accusingly. 'What you said to me in Norfolk made me think you understood. I couldn't wait to share it with you. But obviously I didn't want anyone else to know yet. Not until Parents' Evening. I wanted to reveal it all to my father then! And all the time you thought I was a terrorist. I can't believe you could think that.'

'Sorry.' I gazed into my hot chocolate. 'But, well, there was so much evidence.' I flailed around madly trying to think of some and it all seemed flimsy. Finally I mumbled, 'We kept seeing a strange hooded figure, communicating with you.'

Vlad blushed.

'That person is nothing to do with me,' he said sharply. 'She is to do with you, in fact. I now see, you sent her to spy on me.'

'WHAT?'

'You know that was your friend, Viola, surely?'

Oh. No.

'Viola?'

'Yes. I kept seeing that figure too and I thought it was

someone planning to burgle our house. So last night I lay in wait. And pulled the hood off. She ran away crying.'

'Oh, poor Viola. I had no idea. She didn't mean any harm. She's just . . . fond of you.'

'Oh,' said Vlad, thinking about this. 'So you didn't send her?'

'No. I promise.'

'And that hooded figure was enough to make you think I was a terrorist?' Vlad was scornful.

'No. Of course not. There was the poisoned pond. And the explosion. And the maps . . .'

'What maps?'

'On your wall,' I blurted. Callum kicked me fiercely under the table.

'My wall? You've been in my room?'

Callum interrupted quickly, telling him about Ludmilla's cat getting stuck and how we'd gone to help with Vlad's kitten.

'Ah!' said Vlad and, quite unexpectedly, he burst out laughing. 'I see! I am a spooky Russian, with a mad chemical laboratory. There is a mystery explosion at my flats. The pool is poisoned. Then you discover I have a laboratory in my flat and you put two and two together.'

'Exactly,' I said, relieved.

'But the trouble is, you put two and two together and you make five,' he said. 'That is the trouble with English science, you don't learn it properly. Not at all.

You know the explosion was a gas leak. The pictures of Buckingham Palace, like everything else on my wall, were to highlight important areas of water with bird life, which may give a clue to other breeding grounds for possible algae. I was hoping to send my results to the Queen, actually. Although why you English still want to have a queen is beyond me. You should cut off her head,' he said.

'I'm sure Ms Parker will send it to the Queen,' I said. 'And Callum will do diagrams for you, for Parents' Evening, won't you, Callum? To make up?'

'A-a-achoooo!' was all Callum could say. A waitress came over, having apparently only just noticed that she had three half-drowned customers.

'Look at my floor,' she grumbled. 'Get him to bed.'

We did our best for the Parents' Evening display – but Viola was even further down in the dumps since she'd discovered Vlad was leaving at the end of term because his dad was being posted to the Arctic Circle. I certainly wasn't going to let her know that I knew she had been stalking Vlad. I felt really sorry for her.

'I don't think I'll ever meet anyone like him again,' she said to me sadly. 'He's in a world of his own, isn't he?'

'Well, I think he's trying to make our world better, actually,' I said. 'But he's not husband material, Viola. Never will be.' She looked sadder than ever.When we got to school, we found the hall transformed for the global warming display. Old Frosty and Parky must've been up all night. Frosty had a jolly green hat on and Parky was dressed up as a windmill (don't ask). We were supposed to be in fancy dress as trees and newts and stuff, or at the very least wear something green, so my velvet dress and Candice's posh green wellies came in handy. Viola's crown of woven leaves, with her long face, made her look like a horse stuck in a hedge, but Parky said she looked beautiful, 'like Hamlet's Ophelia'. Tobylerone's friend, Snort, had died his hoodie green, apparently using his face to mix the dye and Tobylerone came as the Jolly Green Recycling Giant in a chain mail thingy made of cans of sweetcorn. He clanked about, slow and sweaty. 'Perhaps you should have used empty tins, Toby,' I couldn't help commenting.

The Parents Association had stalls selling what they called 'locally resourced' and 'organic' foods, although I know for sure that snobby Sasha's mum got her fairy cakes at Marks and Spencer because I saw her chucking the packet in the bin outside the school. 'Roll up, roll up, all proceeds to the Wildlife Garden,' she bellowed.

My heart sank when I saw the work all the other kids had done while I was chasing around after Vlad the Lad. It showed what an inspiration old Nosy Parker had turned out to be. A real legend.

Eric Cubicle had made a huge windmill out of matchsticks. He had a jug of water which he poured on to a little lever at its base and the windmill turned wonkily round. Everyone cheered. 'To demonstrate alternative energy sources, Miss. And it doubles as a ride.' He'd put little baskets on the wheels full of kids made out of Play-Doh.

Tobylerone and Snort's wasteland was papier mâché and littered with old bits of chewing gum and sweet wrappers, skeletons and bones. 'It's showing what would happen if there was no ozone layer left, Miss. See? Everyone's burnt to a crisp and shrivelled up because they couldn't be bothered to turn off the light, Miss.'

'Very effective, Toby, if a touch gruesome,' was Parky's response.

Poor old Parky turned green herself when she saw Jolene and Zandra staggering in with a huge bin bag of rubbish that they emptied on to the nearest display table.

'Girls!' she shrieked, on the verge of tears. But we all love Parky now, and even Zandra and Jolene weren't trying to diss her.

'Nah, Miss. It's not what it looks like. We've chosen the rubbish really carefully, look. It's like an installation, like in the art galleries. It's about what an average teenager has in their room over one week. We did research. Honest.'

Sure enough, every bit of junk was labelled and it was quite scary. Mouldy paper cups, drinks cans, pizza boxes, burger cartons, sweet wrappers and a few things not suitable to mention in a family book such as this.

'I'm glad we're not teenagers yet, Miss, because our rooms are never going to look like this,' said Zandra and Jolene, nodding and smiling like the terrible twins. They'd dressed in identical bottle green mini-skirts and feather boas so it was like watching talking broccoli.

'See? None of the stuff most kids eat is grown locally. None of it is organic . . .'

'Or even food at all,' murmured Parky.

'It's really made us think about what we eat, and the state of the planet, and all the packaging we don't need . . .'

The twin broccolis jabberred on and on and I almost believed them.

Viola's and my project was a disaster. What with Viola's tragic heartbreak and my obsession with spying on Vlad and writing Jane Bond, we wound up with a book that could've been done by a couple of nursery kids, especially since we had to put it on the table next to Mathadi and Lucy's expert model car that they said could run on cat poo. Our book was really lame. I kicked myself when I saw how seriously everyone else had taken it all, knowing Candice was going to be upset by the hoodies and banshees doing so much better than me.

'You might have made a little more effort with your

writing, especially since you are both so good at English,' said Parky, glancing at the big pages with very few words on each of them and the pictures I'd downloaded from the internet in about five minutes. 'Viola's bad ankle has obviously drained her energy, so it's understandable, but you, Cordelia, have done the bare minimum.' I blushed at Viola's and my weedy little project.

By three-thirty, everyone had put their projects out on the tables and there was still no sign of Vlad. Had he chickened out? Maybe I'd been right all along and he was using this very day to skive off school and go to poison the Queen.

Viola's eyes flitted towards the entrance to the hall every few seconds but at four he still hadn't come and parents started pouring into the hall oohing and aahing and pretending to love the weak tea and stale fairy cakes.

Parky clapped her hands together to get everyone's attention, when she thought everyone had spent all the money they were going to spend.

'Welcome to our global warming display. I know you'll agree that all the students have worked very hard,' she said, 'and produced some absolutely magnificent ideas. And as a special surprise we are now having a small talk by our top chemistry student, who showed me his work earlier this morning. I was so impressed that I thought he deserved a little space all of his own. Mr Frost, the curtain, if you please!'

We all turned to look down the hall at the stage. The curtain swooshed open and there was Vlad! In a suit and a green bow tie!

'Thank you so much,' he said, bowing slightly to massive applause and wolf whistles from all the banshees.

He spoke to the assembly just like a prize-winning scientist, with a proper PowerPoint presentation and everything.

I couldn't follow all of it – it was an incredibly detailed account of how our local water supply had been polluted by algae similar to those on the Norfolk broads. They were partly carried by birds, but mostly they'd multiplied due to weather conditions caused by global warming!

'Nutrients from farm chemicals and sewerage have been poured into the Norfolk Broads,' explained Vlad, more animated than I'd ever seen him, 'allowing these microscopic blue-green algae to grow. They've made the water cloudy, causing havoc to the natural system.'

Everyone gasped and applauded his PowerPoint demonstration, packed with masses of chemical formulae, aerial photographs, maps, birds, fish, frogspawn . . . Viola gazed at Vlad in awe, her face a picture of devotion even though I'm not sure she or any of the parents understood any more than I did.

As I listened I became aware of Lucy sobbing quietly somewhere in the region of my knees.

I patted her head.

'It's the frog. I know I killed it. The planet needs frogs,' she hiccupped.

'No. I saw it later. Didn't I tell you? The frog was fine,' I lied.

Vlad finished his speech with a plea for more science in schools, for more care for the planet, for more awareness for everyone. He said science could change the world for the better, as long as scientists were dedicated to saving humanity and the animal kingdom. I thought of Blue, swimming alone in his tank. I thought how my Jane Bond villain was an evil scientist. I thought I should rethink everything. But most of all I thought, Vlad is a really clever guy.

So if one day you see Vladimir Vyshinsky has won the Nobel Prize for science, remember you read it here first.

As I clapped and cheered with everyone else, I had an image of his room. I thought how lucky I was to have seen it, like meeting Beethoven's piano, or Leonardo da Vinci's paintbrush.

Then I remembered he'd had a photo of me on his wall!

All my fears flooded back in a rush. Maybe he had tried to push me under the lorry after all? I could feel myself falling over in the street again. Had he been intending to drown me under the chestnut tree – and only been stopped by Callum being there?

Everyone was cheering like mad and, I thought, this is

how it can happen. People think really bad people are good – and they follow them and vote for them. Like Hitler.

I couldn't get the idea out of my head. I had to know.

After he'd won the prize and been congratulated by everyone I stayed behind to help clear up. Viola's folks had taken her home because her ankle was still playing up.

I hung around pretending to stack chairs. Vlad was packing away his computer, helped by a tall dark man whose vast domed forehead and pointed ears reminded me of Mr Spock from *Star Trek*. I seized my moment when Spock left the hall with the computer.

Vlad took one look at my face and his own fell.

'Didn't you like my presentation?'

'I did. I did. It was brilliant. But . . .'

We were interrupted by Mr Spock, hurrying back in to help again.

Vladimir looked tortured then. Staring at his feet he said, 'This is my father, Ivan Vyshinsky. This is Cordelia.'

'Lucinda Arbuthnott,' finished his dad. 'I am very pleased to meet you. I have heard so much about you.' He smiled broadly and held out his tentacle.

Vlad threw him a withering look and Spock gave a little bow. 'I'll wait outside,' he said.

His dad had heard all about me. My suspicions were confirmed.

'How does your dad know my name? You did try to push me under that lorry, didn't you?'

'You know I didn't. You know I saved you! I told Viola!' shouted Vlad.

'Why have you got my picture on your wall? Where did you get it?'

'From the class photo, of course. Isn't it obvious why?'

And of course it suddenly was. That was why he never talked to the other girls. He had a crush on me!

I stood with my mouth flapping open.

'Sorry,' I said.

'It's OK,' said Vlad. 'We're off to Artic Circle next week. Can I write to you?'

I'm not sure if I nodded or not. I couldn't stop him writing, anyway, could I?

'Maybe you'll have changed in a few years. I can wait,' said Vlad. And then he turned and followed his father into the night.

Callum was waiting for me outside school.

'I won!' he said.

'Won what?'

'You don't care. I just told Viola and she didn't seem to know what I was talking about! She just went blithering on about Vlad the Lad and his fab speech . . .'

'Well, what are you talking about?'

'The "Young Artists Save the Planet" competition! I've won a weekend in Florence, to look at great paintings and stuff.'

'Oh Cal, that's really great. Let's celebrate in the tree house.'

And so Callum and I climbed up the ladder wobbling our mugs of hot chocolate, and snuggled down for a good old chat and a read of my book, like we have been doing for so many years.

'This is happiness,' I thought. 'I'm too young for love.'

I didn't tell Callum what I'd discovered about Vlad liking me. It seemed like boasting somehow. And anyway, it's typical of life that I'm just not ready for love, whereas Viola is ready as anything. Callum's ready too, despite being so small and squeaky. It takes us all at different times I guess. Callum really likes Viola, I can see that. But she doesn't even notice him. Maybe she will one day, if only he could grow another couple of inches and his voice would break . . .

And maybe, one day, if Vlad ever visits again I'll like him in that way. But he'll probably be married by then to a Nobel Prize winner or something.

But there is one thing I do know, and that is that I'm not going to tell Viola what Vlad said either; I don't think she could bear it.

Whatever, I don't think any of us will ever forget Vladimir Vyshinsky.

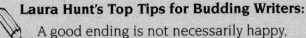

Laura Hunt's Top Tips for Budding Writers:
A good ending is not necessarily happy,
but it should be satisfying and should
also imply that life will continue.
In this way, you keep the illusion that
your characters are real people.

But what if you want to bump your characters off?

The Girl with the Golden Pun (ctd)

Jane Bond awoke yet again with a start, her face stinging. Instead of being boiled in gold, she had been drenched in something freezing. Hunky stood over her, slapping her cheeks violently.

'Quick! We have four minutes until we are blasted to Kingdom come,' he said, as he swiftly cut the extremely slender, but exceptionally strong, golden chains which bound Bond's strong slim ankles.

There was no time to discover how Hunky had rescued her, only the swift realisation that as well as having golden hair and dark honey eyes and shiny biceps, he was on her side after all.

'Where are we?'

'In Goldfumble's rocket. We must divert its course

to Geneva and defuse the bomb!'

Bond snapped into action, wriggling after Hunky through a series of pipes and up and down several ladders and through a variety of complicated hatches until they found themselves in the rocket's control room.

Aurelia Goldfangler was sat at the controls, clad only in a gold satin bikini, a gold chiffon Zandra Rhodes scarf and a pair of Louis Vuitton gold mock crocodile thigh length boots, the robot cat purring innocently on her lap.

She turned – amazed to see Jane Bond silhouetted in the doorway.

'What? But you boiled in the gold! Enough of these unnecessarily complicated and ludicrously easy to elude plot devices! She must be wearing an asbestos suit!'

'No, Aurelia,' said Hunky, emerging from behind Bond, his dark honey eyes glinting in the strange fluorescent light of the rocket's cockpit. 'It was not a vat of boiling gold at all. It was merely gold paint. I changed it while you were with your stupid cat.'

'What? How dare you call my Zanzibar stupid?' said Goldbangle, her lip trembling.

'He is nothing but a robot,' sneered Hunky, grabbing Zanzibar by the tail. 'Listen!'

He pushed a switch in Zanzibar's collar and a tape recording of everything that Goldfumble had done for the last four weeks echoed round the cockpit.

'My own cat and my own Hunky have betrayed me!' cried

Goldfumble, shrinking to a shadow of her former self.

Hunky pushed a pellet of compressed air into Goldfangler's mouth until she swallowed it, and pushed her into the hold.

'It will make her explode shortly,' he told Bond. 'Meanwhile we must change the rocket's course to Geneva.'

Hunky swiftly pressed some buttons and pulled a few important-looking shiny levers while Goldbungler swelled to eight times her usual size.

'That should show her the error of her weighs,' quipped Bond, feeling it was time for a pun.

Goldfarbler exploded with a loud bang.

'She always did have an inflated opinion of herself,' smiled Bond, brushing Hunky's golden hair with her lips.

Seconds later they landed in Geneva and defused Goldfumble 's bomb with seconds to spare.

'Thank goodness you had that gun with the Swiss army thing,' said Hunky, panting slightly.

'I am off to dig my allotment now,' said Bond. 'Do you want to come?'

'Certainly,' said Hunky, smiling his hunky smile.

But a bayonetted boot shot out from behind a rock and pierced him fatally through the heart.

Just my luck, thought Bond. Midas has survived! This always happens whenever I find a man who might be able to whip up a decent omelette.

Jane Bond was alone, facing Goldfumble's one-legged, steel-toothed, metal-rimmed bowler-hatted, bayonet-booted ruthless sidekick and hired assassin, whose cruelty knew no bounds.

'Fool!' sneered Dr. Midas. 'I have a second device here in my hand that will blow us all up!'

But Bond, who had not yet had a chance to use her kung fu or all of her gadgets, used most of them all at once and sliced off Midas's right arm in a trice.

'Ooh, I never knew I could be so disarming,' she said, as Dr Midas hopped about in pain on his bayonetted boot.

'Hah! But I have a spare device here!' shrieked the evil assassin, waving his left hand which held another bombing device and simultaneously flicking his head so that his metal-rimmed bowler hat flew with deadly precision towards Bond, threatening to slice off her head. She ducked, swiftly fitting a boomerang device on to the hat as it whizzed past her ear.

Almost in slow motion, the hat made a graceful circle and flew back to its unsuspecting owner, who caught it in his metal teeth, unaware that the crafty boomerang device was in fact also an explosive, which swiftly blew him to smithereens.

'His arm! Watch out for his arm!' gasped Hunky, who was lying nearby in a pool of blood, gasping his last.

Bond looked down at Midas's severed right arm, twitching slightly on the cave floor.

'Heavens! It is still clutching the bomb, and it is about to go off!'

There were ten seconds ticking away on the timer.

Bond fearlessly picked it up. But it was not the same kind of fuse that she was used to.

'Hunky, do you understand this fuse?'

'Oh Jane, Jane, I think I am dying . . .'

'Yes, but tell me about the fuse.'

'Press the red button on the right, or the green button on the left, I'm not sure which.'

There were two seconds to go. Bond would have to choose. Red means stop, she thought to herself. And green means go. But I expect Midas would have done it differently to confuse us. I'll take a chance.

Bravely, she pressed the green button. Silence.

'You've done it,' said Hunky. 'Will you marry me?'

'It may be a case of wife or death,' quipped Bond, stroking Hunky's now limp golden locks. 'Can you make a good omelette?"

'No,' said Hunky, with his dying breath, and, in Goldbungler's vast underground cavern, littered with the grisly remains of Dr Midas, Hunky expired.

Bond reached for her mobile and phoned Z.

'Congratulations, Bond. Can you report to us tomorrow at 0700 hours? There's another little mission I have in mind. Unfortunately it seems Goldflinger had a sister, twice as nasty as she was . . .'

Bond gazed regretfully at the dead hunk that had once been Hunky Misterson.

It is sad, she thought. But it would never have worked. I'm not really the marrying kind.

'OK, Z,' she said. 'I'll be there.'

Laura Hunt's Top Tips for Budding Writers:
No one believes in 'happily ever after',
except in fairy stories.

What kind of tip is that?
Have you ever actually read a story that ends that way?

Girl Writer

Ros Asquith

Castles and Catastrophes

Cordelia Arbuthnott wants to write books. Not the sort that her aunt, the bestselling children's author Laura Hunt writes, but literary masterpieces.

So when she finds out that her dreaded new school Falmer North is having a writing competition, she's delighted. She just knows her medieval love story, *The Lady of the Rings*, will win the romance category.

But writing a masterpiece is trickier than she expected. What with wanting to make a good impression at Falmer North, sorting out her best friend Callum's home problems, and coping with her eccentric family, real life just keeps getting in the way.

'Couldn't put it down. Must have Pritt Stick on my paws.'
Xerxes, the author's cat

'Cordelia writes so well she makes me feel I should put the quill back in my ostrich.'
JK Rolling

ISBN: 978 1 85340 823 9

Girl Writer

Ros Asquith

Sleuths and Truths

Cordelia Arbuthnott is determined to become a world famous author and her latest passion is writing the adventures of Shirley Holmes, Sherlock's younger sister. But as she gets stuck into *The Bat of the D'Urbervilles*, her interest in a real life mystery involving her schoolmate, Viola, deepens.

With the help of her best friend Callum, she discovers that Viola's dad is in jail for bank robbery. Cordelia is convinced he's not the real culprit and the three of them are determined to prove his innocence. But are they right?

Packed with top tips for aspiring writers, this is the second book in Ros Asquith's hilarious *Girl Writer* series.

'Undoubtedly the best book ever about an aspiring girl writer searching for justice in a cruel world.'
Prof Arbuthnott, BA Hons, MA

'A truly fishy tale with something for everyone, even me.'
Blue, the author's goldfish

ISBN: 978 1 85340 910 3

Try out some other Piccadilly Pearls books!

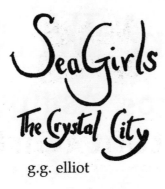

Sea Girls
The Crystal City

g.g. elliot

As Polly dived into the pool, the water went straight up her nose. Normally this would make her choke and gasp for air, but this time some instinct made her suck the water through her nose and push it out of her mouth. She could breathe underwater!

Even before this, Polly had always felt different. But then she finds a kindred spirit in Lisa, who she meets at a swimming competition. The two girls discover that they both have the same fish-shaped birthmark, were both adopted, and can both breathe underwater. Surely it can't just be coincidence?

When a strong current drags them to the depths of the ocean, they not only discover their true identities, but an amazing world – more incredible and more disturbing than they could ever have imagined . . .

'It's got mystery, a magical new world and it's got excitement oozing from its gills.' Liverpool Echo

ISBN: 978 1 85340 878 6

Stunt ★ Girl

JONNY ZUCKER

Venus leapt from the platform like a springing cheetah, pumping her legs in mid-air as she'd seen long-jumpers do. There were gasps from the people below – there was no way she could make it across without a rope. She hung in the air as if suspended, as if for a second she'd bypassed the laws of time and gravity.

Venus Spring is fourteen and this is the first summer she'd been allowed to go to stunt camp. It is a dream come true, something she has been working towards for years. But while she is there, she stumbles on a devious and terrifying plot that threatens the surrounding countryside, and Venus is determined to uncover it.

'*An exciting page-turner that will have you gripped!*' MIZZ

'*A fast-paced, thrilling read.*' The Sunday Times

ISBN: 978 1 85340 837 3

Cherry Whytock

Honeysuckle Lovelace

The Dog Walkers' Club

There comes a time in almost everybody's life when they have a brilliant idea. Honeysuckle Lovelace's Brilliant Idea is to set up a Dog Walkers' Club with her friends. She can spend time with her favourite animals *and* earn some money to help mend the leaky houseboat where she and her mum live.

The club's first 'client' is Cupid, Mrs Whitely-Grub's pinky-white poodle, who barely even passes for a dog. As Cupid becomes a regular client, Honeysuckle is increasingly suspicious of his owner. She's determined to solve the mysteries surrounding Mrs Whitely-Grub – and the Dog Walkers' Club provides the perfect cover!

ISBN: 978 1 85340 889 2